AFTER THE STORM

T. S. Arthur

1st WORLD
LIBRARY
Literary Society

After the Storm

T. S. Arthur

© 1st World Library – Literary Society, 2004
PO Box 2211
Fairfield, IA 52556
www.1stworldlibrary.org
First Edition

LCCN: 2004195360

Softcover ISBN: 1-4218-0194-9
Hardcover ISBN: 1-4218-0094-2
eBook ISBN: 1-4218-0294-5

Purchase *"After the Shadow"*
as a traditional bound book at:
www.1stWorldLibrary.org/purchase.asp?ISBN=1-4218-0194-9

1st World Library Literary Society is a nonprofit organization dedicated to promoting literacy by:

- Creating a free internet library accessible from any computer worldwide.
- Hosting writing competitions and offering book publishing scholarships.

Readers interested in supporting literacy through sponsorship, donations or membership please contact:
literacy@1stworldlibrary.org
Check us out at: www.1stworldlibrary.ORG
and start downloading free ebooks today.

After the Storm
contributed by Tim, Ed & Rodney
in support of
1st World Library Literary Society

CONTENTS

CHAPTER I

THE WAR OF THE ELEMENTS.

NO June day ever opened with a fairer promise. Not a single cloud flecked the sky, and the sun coursed onward through the azure sea until past meridian, without throwing to the earth a single shadow. Then, low in the west, appeared something obscure and hazy, blending the hill-tops with the horizon; an hour later, and three or four small fleecy islands were seen, clearly outlined in the airy ocean, and slowly ascending - avant-couriers of a coming storm. Following these were mountain peaks, snow-capped and craggy, with desolate valleys between. Then, over all this arctic panorama, fell a sudden shadow. The white tops of the cloudy hills lost their clear, gleaming outlines and their slumbrous stillness. The atmosphere was in motion, and a white scud began to drive across the heavy, dark masses of clouds that lay far back against the sky in mountain-like repose.

How grandly now began the onward march of the tempest, which had already invaded the sun's domain and shrouded his face in the smoke of approaching battle. Dark and heavy it lay along more than half the visible horizon, while its crown invaded the zenith.

As yet, all was silence and portentous gloom. Nature

seemed to pause and hold her breath in dread anticipation. Then came a muffled, jarring sound, as of far distant artillery, which died away into an oppressive stillness. Suddenly from zenith to horizon the cloud was cut by a fiery stroke, an instant visible. Following this, a heavy thunder-peal shook the solid earth, and rattled in booming echoes along the hillsides and amid the cloudy caverns above.

At last the storm came down on the wind's strong pinions, swooping fiercely to the earth, like an eagle to its prey. For one wild hour it raged as if the angel of destruction were abroad.

At the window of a house standing picturesquely among the Hudson Highlands, and looking down upon the river, stood a maiden and her lover, gazing upon this wild war among the elements. Fear had pressed her closely to his side, and he had drawn an arm around her in assurance of safety.

Suddenly the maiden clasped her hands over her face, cried out and shuddered. The lightning had shivered a tree upon which her gaze was fixed, rending it as she could have rent a willow wand.

"God is in the storm," said the lover, bending to her ear. He spoke reverently and in a voice that had in it no tremor of fear.

The maiden withdrew her hands from before her shut eyes, and looking up into his face, answered in a voice which she strove to make steady:

"Thank you, Hartley, for the words. Yes, God is present in the storm, as in the sunshine."

"Look!" exclaimed the young man, suddenly, pointing to the river. A boat had just come in sight. It contained a man and a woman. The former was striving with a pair of oars to keep the boat right in the eye of the wind; but while the maiden and her lover still gazed at them, a wild gust swept down upon the water and drove their frail bark under. There was no hope in their case; the floods had swallowed them, and would not give up their living prey.

A moment afterward, and an elm, whose great arms had for nearly a century spread themselves out in the sunshine tranquilly or battled with the storms, fell crashing against the house, shaking it to the very foundations.

The maiden drew back from the window, overcome with terror. These shocks were too much for her nerves. But her lover restrained her, saying, with a covert chiding in his voice,

"Stay, Irene! There is a wild delight in all this, and are you not brave enough to share it with me?"

But she struggled to release herself from his arm, replying with a shade of impatience -

"Let me go, Hartley! Let me go!"

The flexed arm was instantly relaxed, and the maiden was free. She went back, hastily, from the window, and, sitting down on a sofa, buried her face in her hands. The young man did not follow her, but remained standing by the window, gazing out upon Nature in her strong convulsion. It may, however, be doubted whether his mind took note of the wild images that were pictured in his eyes. A cloud was in the horizon of his mind, dimming its heavenly azure. And the maiden's sky was shadowed also.

For two or three minutes the young man stood by the window, looking out at the writhing trees and the rain pouring down an avalanche of water, and then, with a movement that indicated a struggle and a conquest, turned and walked toward the sofa on which the maiden still sat with her face hidden from view. Sitting down beside her, he took her hand. It lay passive in his. He pressed it gently; but she gave back no returning pressure. There came a sharp, quick gleam of lightning, followed by a crash that jarred the house. But Irene did not start - we may question whether she even saw the one or heard the other, except as something remote.

"Irene!"

She did not stir.

The young man leaned closer, and said, in a tender voice -

"Irene - darling -"

Her hand moved in his - just moved - but did not return the pressure of his own.

"Irene." And now his arm stole around her. She yielded, and, turning, laid her head upon his shoulder.

There had been a little storm in the maiden's heart, consequent upon the slight restraint ventured on by her lover when she drew back from the window; and it was

T. S. Arthur

only now subsiding.

"I did not mean to offend you," said the young man, penitently.

"Who said that I was offended?" She looked up, with a smile that only half obliterated the shadow. "I was frightened, Hartley. It is a fearful storm!" And she glanced toward the window.

The lover accepted this affirmation, though he knew better in his heart. He knew that his slight attempt at constraint had chafed her naturally impatient spirit, and that it had taken her some time to regain her lost self-control.

Without, the wild rush of winds was subsiding, the lightning gleamed out less frequently, and the thunder rolled at a farther distance. Then came that deep stillness of nature which follows in the wake of the tempest, and in its hush the lovers stood again at the window, looking out upon the wrecks that were strewn in its path. They were silent, for on both hearts was a shadow, which had not rested there when they first stood by the window, although the sky was then more deeply veiled. So slight was the cause on which these shadows depended that memory scarcely retained its impression. He was tender, and she was yielding; and each tried to atone by loving acts for a moment of willfulness.

The sun went down while yet the skirts of the storm were spread over the western sky, and without a single glance at the ruins which lightning, wind and rain had scattered over the earth's fair surface. But he arose gloriously in the coming morning, and went upward in his strength, consuming the vapors at a breath, and drinking up every bright dewdrop that welcomed him with a quiver of joy. The branches shook themselves in the gentle breezes his presence had called forth to dally amid their foliage and sport with the flowers; and every green thing put on a fresher beauty in delight at his return; while from the bosom of the trees - from hedgerow and from meadow - went up the melody of birds.

In the brightness of this morning, the lovers went out to look at the storm-wrecks that lay scattered around. Here a tree had been twisted off where the tough wood measured by feet instead of inches; there stood the white and shivered trunk of another sylvan lord, blasted in an instant by a lightning stroke; and there lay, prone upon the ground, giant limbs, which, but the day before, spread themselves abroad in proud defiance of the storm. Vines were torn from their fastenings; flower-beds destroyed; choice shrubbery, tended with care for years, shorn of its beauty. Even the solid earth had been invaded by floods of water, which ploughed deep furrows along its surface. And, saddest of all, two human lives had gone out while the mad tempest raged in uncontrollable fury.

As the lover and maiden stood looking at the signs of violence so thickly scattered around, the former said, in a cheerful tone -

"For all his wild, desolating power, the tempest is vassal to the sun and dew. He may spread his sad trophies around in brief, blind rage; but they soon obliterate all traces of his path, and make beautiful what he has scarred with wounds or disfigured by the tramp of his iron heel."

T. S. Arthur

"Not so, my children," said the calm voice of the maiden's father, to whose ears the remark had come. "Not so, my children. The sun and dew never fully restore what the storm has broken and trampled upon. They may hide disfiguring marks, and cover with new forms of life and beauty the ruins which time can never restore. This is something, and we may take the blessing thankfully, and try to forget what is lost, or so changed as to be no longer desirable. Look at this fallen and shattered elm, my children. Is there any hope for that in the dew, the rain and sunshine? Can these build it up again, and spread out its arms as of old, bringing back to me, as it has done daily, the image of my early years? No, my children. After every storm are ruins which can never be repaired. Is it not so with that lightning-stricken oak? And what art can restore to its exquisite loveliness this statue of Hope, thrown down by the ruthless hand of the unsparing tempest? Moreover, is there human vitality in the sunshine and fructifying dew? Can they put life into the dead?

"No - no - my children. And take the lesson to heart. Outward tempests but typify and represent the fiercer tempests that too often desolate the human soul. In either case something is lost that can never be restored. Beware, then, of storms, for wreck and ruin follow as surely as the passions rage."

CHAPTER II.

THE LOVERS.

IRENE DELANCY was a girl of quick, strong feelings, and an undisciplined will. Her mother died before she reached her tenth year. From that time she was either at home under the care of domestics, or within the scarcely more favorable surroundings of a boarding-school. She grew up beautiful and accomplished, but capricious and with a natural impatience of control, that unwise reactions on the part of those who attempted to govern her in no degree tempered.

Hartley Emerson, as a boy, was self-willed and passionate, but possessed many fine qualities. A weak mother yielded to his resolute struggles to have his own way, and so he acquired, at an early age, control over his own movements. He went to college, studied hard, because he was ambitious, and graduated with honor. Law he chose as a profession; and, in order to secure the highest advantages, entered the office of a distinguished attorney in the city of New York, and gave to its study the best efforts of a clear, acute and logical mind. Self-reliant, proud, and in the habit of reaching his ends by the nearest ways, he took his place at the bar with a promise of success rarely exceeded. From his widowed mother, who died before he reached his majority, Hartley Emerson inherited a moderate fortune with which to begin the world. Few young men started forward on their life-journey with so small a number of vices, or with so spotless a moral character. The fine intellectual cast of his mind, and his devotion to study, lifted him above the baser allurements of sense and kept his garments pure.

Such were Irene Delancy and Hartley Emerson - lovers and betrothed at the time we present them to our readers. They met, two years before, at Saratoga, and drew together by a mutual attraction. She was the first to whom his heart had bowed in homage; and until she looked upon him her pulse had never beat quicker at sight of a manly form.

Mr. Edmund Delancy, a gentleman of some wealth and advanced in years, saw no reason to interpose objections. The family of Emerson occupied a social position equal with his own; and the young man's character and habits were blameless. So far, the course of love ran smooth; and only three months intervened until the wedding-day.

The closer relation into which the minds of the lovers came after their betrothal and the removal of a degree of deference and self-constraint, gave opportunity for the real character of each to show itself. Irene could not always repress her willfulness and impatience of another's control; nor her lover hold a firm hand on quick-springing anger when anything checked his purpose. Pride and adhesiveness of character, under such conditions of mind, were dangerous foes to peace; and both were proud and tenacious.

The little break in the harmonious flow of their lives, noticed as occurring while the tempest raged, was one of many such incidents; and it was in consequence of Mr. Delancy's observation of these unpromising features in their intercourse that he spoke with so much earnestness about the irreparable ruin that followed in the wake of storms.

At least once a week Emerson left the city, and his books and cases, to spend a day with Irene in her tasteful home; and sometimes he lingered there for two or three days at a time. It happened, almost invariably, that some harsh notes jarred in the music of their lives during these pleasant seasons, and left on both their hearts a feeling of oppression, or, worse, a brooding sense of injustice. Then there grew up between them an affected opposition and indifference, and a kind of half-sportive, half-earnest wrangling about trifles, which too often grew serious.

Mr. Delancy saw this with a feeling of regret, and often interposed to restore some broken links in the chain of harmony.

"You must be more conciliating, Irene," he would often say to his daughter. "Hartley is earnest and impulsive, and you should yield to him gracefully, even when you do not always see and feel as he does. This constant opposition and standing on your dignity about trifles is fretting both of you, and bodes evil in the future."

"Would you have me assent if he said black was white?" she answered to her father's remonstrance one day, balancing her little head firmly and setting her lips together in a resolute way.

"It might be wiser to say nothing than to utter dissent,

T. S. Arthur

if, in so doing, both were made unhappy," returned her father.

"And so let him think me a passive fool?" she asked.

"No; a prudent girl, shaming his unreasonableness by her self-control."

"I have read somewhere," said Irene, "that all men are self-willed tyrants - the words do not apply to you, my father, and so there is an exception to the rule." She smiled a tender smile as she looked into the face of a parent who had ever been too indulgent. "But, from my experience with a lover, I can well believe the sentiment based in truth. Hartley must have me think just as he thinks, and do what he wants me to do, or he gets ruffled. Now I don't expect, when I am married, to sink into a mere nobody - to be my husband's echo and shadow; and the quicker I can make Hartley comprehend this the better will it be for both of us. A few rufflings of his feathers now will teach him how to keep them smooth and glossy in the time to come."

"You are in error, my child," replied Mr. Delancy, speaking very seriously. "Between those who love a cloud should never interpose; and I pray you, Irene, as you value your peace and that of the man who is about to become your husband, to be wise in the very beginning, and dissolve with a smile of affection every vapor that threatens a coming storm. Keep the sky always bright."

"I will do everything that I can, father, to keep the sky of our lives always bright, except give up my own freedom of thought and independence of action. A wife should not sink her individuality in that of her husband, any more than a husband should sink his individuality in that of his wife. They are two equals, and should be content to remain equals. There is no love in subordination."

Mr. Delancy sighed deeply: "Is argument of any avail here? Can words stir conviction in her mind?" He was silent for a time, and then said -

"Better, Irene, that you stop where you are, and go through life alone, than venture upon marriage, in your state of feeling, with a man like Hartley Emerson."

"Dear father, you are altogether too serious!" exclaimed the warm-hearted girl, putting her arms around his neck and kissing him. "Hartley and I love each other too well to be made very unhappy by any little jar that takes place in the first reciprocal movement of our lives. We shall soon come to understand each other, and then the harmonies will be restored."

"The harmonies should never be lost, my child," returned Mr. Delancy. "In that lies the danger. When the enemy gets into the citadel, who can say that he will ever be dislodged? There is no safety but in keeping him out."

"Still too serious, father," said Irene. "There is no danger to be feared from any formidable enemy. All these are very little things."

"It is the little foxes that spoil the tender grapes, my daughter," Mr. Delancy replied; "and if the tender grapes are spoiled, what hope is there in the time of vintage? Alas for us if in the later years the wine of life shall fail!"

There was so sad a tone in her father's voice, and so sad an expression on his face, that Irene was touched with a new feeling toward him. She again put her arms around his neck and kissed him tenderly.

"Do not fear for us," she replied. "These are only little summer showers, that make the earth greener and the flowers more beautiful. The sky is of a more heavenly azure when they pass away, and the sun shines more gloriously than before."

But the father could not be satisfied, and answered -

"Beware of even summer showers, my darling. I have known fearful ravages to follow in their path - seen many a goodly tree go down. After every storm, though the sky may be clearer, the earth upon which it fell has suffered some loss which is a loss for ever. Begin, then, by conciliation and forbearance. Look past the external, which may seem at times too exacting or imperative, and see only the true heart pulsing beneath - the true, brave heart, that would give to every muscle the strength of steel for your protection if danger threatened. Can you not be satisfied with knowing that you are loved - deeply, truly, tenderly? What more can a woman ask? Can you not wait until this love puts on its rightly-adjusted exterior, as it assuredly will. It is yet mingled with self-love, and its action modified by impulse and habit. Wait - wait - wait, my daughter. Bear and forbear for a time, as you value peace on earth and happiness in heaven."

" I will try , father , for your sake, to guard myself,"

she answered.

"No, no, Irene. Not for my sake, but for the sake of right," returned Mr. Delancy.

They were sitting in the vine-covered portico that looked down, over a sloping lawn toward the river.

"There is Hartley now!" exclaimed Irene, as the form of her lover came suddenly into view, moving forward along the road that approached from the landing, and she sprung forward and went rapidly down to meet him. There an ardent kiss, a twining of arms, warmly spoken words and earnest gestures. Mr. Delancy looked at them as they stood fondly together, and sighed. He could not help it, for he knew there was trouble before them. After standing and talking for a short time, they began moving toward the house, but paused at every few paces - sometimes to admire a picturesque view - sometimes to listen one to the other and respond to pleasant sentiments - and sometimes in fond dispute. This was Mr. Delancy's reading of their actions and gestures, as he sat looking at and observing them closely.

A little way from the path by which they were advancing toward the house was a rustic arbor, so placed as to command a fine sweep of river from one line of view and West Point from another. Irene paused and made a motion of her hand toward this arbor, as if she wished to go there; but Hartley looked to the house and plainly signified a wish to go there first. At this Irene pulled him gently toward the arbor; he resisted, and she drew upon his arm more resolutely, when, planting his feet firmly, he stood like a rock. Still she urged and still he declined going in that direction. It was play at first, but Mr. Delancy saw that it was growing to be earnest. A few moments longer, and he saw Irene separate from Hartley and move toward the arbor; at the same time the young man came forward in the direction of the house. Mr. Delancy, as he stepped from the portico to meet him, noticed that his color was heightened and his eyes unusually bright.

"What's the matter with that self-willed girl of mine?" he asked, as he took the hand of Emerson, affecting a lightness of tone that did not correspond with his real feelings.

"Oh, nothing serious," the young man replied. "She's only in a little pet because I wouldn't go with her to the arbor before I paid my respects to you."

"She's a spoiled little puss," said the father, in a fond yet serious way, "and you'll have to humor her a little at first, Hartley. She never had the wise discipline of a mother, and so has grown up unused to that salutary control which is so necessary for young persons. But she has a warm, true heart and pure principles; and these are the foundation-stones on which to build the temple of happiness."

"Don't fear but that it will be all right between us. I love her too well to let any flitting humors affect me."

He stepped upon the portico as he spoke and sat down. Irene had before this reached the arbor and taken a seat there. Mr. Delancy could do no less than resume the chair from which he had arisen on the young man's approach. In looking into Hartley's face he noticed a resolute expression about his mouth. For nearly ten minutes they sat and talked, Irene remaining alone in the arbor. Mr. Delancy then said, in a pleasant off-handed way,

"Come, Hartley, you have punished her long enough. I don't like to see you even play at disagreement."

He did not seem to notice the remark, but started a subject of conversation that it was almost impossible to dismiss for the next ten minutes. Then he stepped down from the portico, and was moving leisurely toward the arbor when he perceived that Irene had already left it and was returning by another path. So he came back and seated himself again, to await her approach. But, instead of joining him, she passed round the house and entered on the opposite side. For several minutes he sat, expecting every instant to see her come out on the portico, but she did not make her appearance.

It was early in the afternoon. Hartley, affecting not to notice the absence of Irene, kept up an animated conversation with Mr. Delancy. A whole hour went by, and still the young lady was absent. Suddenly starting, up, at the end of this time, Hartley exclaimed -

"As I live, there comes the boat! and I must be in New York to-night."

"Stay," said Mr. Delancy, "until I call Irene."

"I can't linger for a moment, sir. It will take quick walking to reach the landing by the time the boat is there." The young man spoke hurriedly, shook hands with Mr. Delancy, and then sprung away, moving at a rapid pace.

T. S. Arthur

"What's the matter, father? Where is Hartley going?" exclaimed Irene, coming out into the portico and grasping her father's arm. Her face was pale and her lips trembled.

"He is going to New York," relied Mr. Delancy.

"To New York!" She looked almost frightened.

"Yes. The boat is coming, and he says that he must be in the city to-night."

Irene sat down, looking pale and troubled.

"Why have you remained away from Hartley ever since his arrival?" asked Mr. Delancy, fixing his eyes upon Irene and evincing some displeasure.

Irene did not answer, but her father saw the color coming back to her face.

"I think, from his manner, that he was hurt by your singular treatment. What possessed you to do so?"

"Because I was not pleased with him," said Irene. Her voice was now steady.

"Why not?"

"I wished him to go to the arbor."

"He was your guest, and, in simple courtesy, if there was no other motive, you should have let his wishes govern your movements," Mr. Delancy replied.

"He is always opposing me!" said Irene, giving way to

a flood of tears and weeping for a time bitterly.

"It is not at all unlikely, my daughter," replied Mr. Delancy, after the tears began to flow less freely, "that Hartley is now saying the same thing of you, and treasuring up bitter things in his heart. I have no idea that any business calls him to New York to-night."

"Nor I. He takes this means to punish me," said Irene.

"Don't take that for granted. Your conduct has blinded him, and he is acting now from blind impulse. Before he is half-way to New York he will regret this hasty step as sincerely as I trust you are already regretting its occasion."

Irene did not reply.

"I did not think," he resumed, "that my late earnest remonstrance would have so soon received an illustration like this. But it may be as well. Trifles light as air have many times proved the beginning of life-longs separations between friends and lovers who possessed all the substantial qualities for a life-long and happy companionship. Oh, my daughter, beware! beware of these little beginnings of discord. How easy would it have been for you to have yielded to Hartley's wishes! - how hard will it to endure the pain that must now be suffered! And remember that you do not suffer alone; your conduct has made him an equal sufferer. He came up all the way from the city full of sweet anticipations. It was for your sake that he came; and love pictured you as embodying all attractions. But how has he found you? Ah, my daughter, your caprice has wounded the heart that turned to you for love. He came in joy, but goes back in sorrow."

T. S. Arthur

Irene went up to her chamber, feeling sadder than she had ever felt in her life; yet, mingling, with her sadness and self-reproaches, were complaining thoughts of her lover. For a little half-playful pettishness was she to be visited with a punishment like this? If be had really loved her - so she queried - would be have flung himself away after this hasty fashion? Pride came to her aid in the conflict of feeling, and gave her self-control and endurance. At tea-time she met her father, and surprised him with her calm, almost cheerful, aspect. But his glance was too keen not to penetrate the disguise. After tea, she sat reading - or at least affecting to read - in the portico, until the evening shadows came down, and then she retired to her chamber.

Not many hours of sleep brought forgetfulness of suffering through the night that followed. Sometimes the unhappy girl heaped mountains of reproaches upon her own head; and sometimes pride and indignation, gaining rule in her heart, would whisper self-justification, and throw the weight of responsibility upon her lover.

Her pale face and troubled eyes revealed too plainly, on the next morning, the conflict through which she had passed.

"Write him a letter of apology or explanation," said Mr. Delancy.

But Irene was not in a state of mind for this. Pride came whispering too many humiliating objections in her ear. Morning passed, and in the early hours of the afternoon, when the New York boat usually came up the river, she was out on the portico watching for its appearance. Hope whispered that, repenting of his hasty return on the day before, her lover was now hurrying back to meet her. At last the white hull of the boat came gliding into view, and in less than half an hour it was at the landing. Then it moved on its course again. Almost to a second of time had Irene learned to calculate the minutes it required for Hartley to make the distance between the landing and the nearest point in the road where his form could meet her view. She held her breath in eager expectation as that moment of time approached. It came - it passed; the white spot in the road, where his dark form first revealed itself, was touched by no obscuring shadow. For more than ten minutes Irene sat motionless, gazing still toward that point; then, sighing deeply, she arose and went up to her room, from which she did not come down until summoned to join her father at tea.

The next day passed as this had done, and so did the next. Hartley neither came nor sent a message of any kind. The maiden's heart began to fail. Grief and fear took the place of accusation and self-reproach. What if he had left her for ever! The thought made her heart shiver as if an icy wind had passed over it. Two or three times she took up her pen to write him a few words and entreat him to come back to her again. But she could form no sentences against which pride did not come with strong objection; and so she suffered on, and made no sign.

A whole week at last intervened. Then the enduring heart began to grow stronger to bear, and, in self-protection, to put on sterner moods. Hers was not a spirit to yield weakly in any struggle. She was formed for endurance, pride and self-reliance giving her strength above common natures. But this did not really

T. S. Arthur

lessen her suffering, for she was not only capable of deep affection, but really loved Hartley almost as her own life; and the thought of losing him, whenever it grew distinct, filled her with terrible anguish.

With pain her father saw the color leave her cheeks, her eyes grow fixed and dreamy, and her lips shrink from their full outline.

"Write to Hartley," he said to her one day, after a week had passed.

"Never!" was her quick, firm, almost sharply uttered response; "I would die first!"

"But, my daughter -"

"Father," she interrupted him, two bright spots suddenly burning on her cheeks, "don't, I pray you, urge me on this point. I have courage enough to break, but I will not bend. I gave him no offence. What right has he to assume that I was not engaged in domestic duties while he sat talking with you? He said that he had an engagement in New York. Very well; there was a sufficient reason for his sudden departure; and I accept the reason. But why does he remain away? If simply because I preferred a seat in the arbor to one in the portico, why, the whole thing is so unmanly, that I can have no patience with it. Write to him, and humor a whim like this! No, no - Irene Delancy is not made of the right stuff. He went from me, and he must return again. I cannot go to him. Maiden modesty and pride forbid. And so I shall remain silent and passive, if my heart breaks."

It was in the afternoon, and they were sitting in the

portico, where, at this hour, Irene might have been found every day for the past week. The boat from New York came in sight as she closed the last sentence. She saw it - for her eyes were on the look-out - the moment it turned the distant point of land that hid the river beyond. Mr. Delancy also observed the boat. Its appearance was an incident of sufficient importance, taking things as they were, to check the conversation, which was far from being satisfactory on either side.

The figure of Irene was half buried in a deep cushioned chair, which had been wheeled out upon the portico, and now her small, slender form seemed to shrink farther back among the cushions, and she sat as motionless as one asleep. Steadily onward came the boat, throwing backward her dusky trail and lashing with her great revolving wheels the quiet waters into foamy turbulence - onward, until the dark crowd of human forms could be seen upon her decks; then, turning sharply, she was lost to view behind a bank of forest trees. Ten minutes more, and the shriek of escaping steam was heard as she stopped her ponderous machinery at the landing.

From that time Irene almost held her breath, as so she counted the moments that must elapse before Hartley could reach the point of view in the road that led up from the river, should he have been a passenger in the steamboat. The number was fully told, but it was to-day as yesterday. There was no sign of his coming. And so the eyelids, weary with vain expectation, drooped heavily over the dimming eyes. But she had not stirred, nor shown a sign of feeling. A little while she sat with her long lashes shading her pale cheeks; then she slowly raised them and looked out toward the river again. What a quick start she gave! Did her eyes deceive her? No, it was Hartley, just in the spot she had looked to see him only a minute or two before. But how slowly he moved, and with what a weary step! and, even at this long distance, his face looked white against the wavy masses of his dark-brown hair.

Irene started up with an exclamation, stood as if in doubt for a moment, then, springing from the portico, she went flying to meet him, as swiftly as if moving on winged feet. All the forces of her ardent, impulsive nature were bearing her forward. There was no remembrance of coldness or imagined wrong - pride did not even struggle to lift its head - love conquered everything. The young man stood still, from weariness or surprise, ere she reached him. As she drew near, Irene saw that his face was not only pale, but thin and wasted.

"Oh, Hartley! dear Hartley!" came almost wildly from her lips, as she flung her arms around his neck, and kissed him over and over again, on lips, cheeks and brow, with an ardor and tenderness that no maiden delicacy could restrain. "Have you been sick, or hurt? Why are you so pale, darling?"

"I have been ill for a week - ever since I was last here," the young man replied, speaking in a slow, tremulous voice.

"And I knew it not!" Tears were glittering in her eyes and pressing out in great pearly beads from between the fringing lashes. "Why did you not send for me, Hartley?"

And she laid her small hands upon each side of his face, as you have seen a mother press the cheeks of her child, and looked up tenderly into his love-beaming eyes.

"But come, dear," she added, removing her hands from his face and drawing her arm within his - not to lean on, but to offer support. "My father, who has, with me, suffered great anxiety on your account, is waiting your arrival at the house."

Then, with slow steps, they moved along the upward sloping way, crowding the moments with loving words.

And so the storm passed, and the sun came out again in the firmament of their souls. But looked he down on no tempest-marks? Had not the ruthless tread of passion marred the earth's fair surface? Were no goodly trees uptorn, or clinging vines wrenched from their support? Alas! was there ever a storm that did not leave some ruined hope behind? ever a storm that did not strew the sea with wrecks or mar the earth's fair beauty?

As when the pain of a crushed limb ceases there comes to the sufferer a sense of delicious ease, so, after the storm had passed, the lovers sat in the warm sunshine and dreamed of unclouded happiness in the future. But in the week that Hartley spent with his betrothed were revealed to their eyes, many times, desolate places where flowers had been; and their hearts grew sad as they turned their eyes away, and sighed for hopes departed, faith shaken, and untroubled confidence in each other for the future before them, for ever gone.

CHAPTER III.

THE CLOUD AND THE SIGN.

IN alternate storm and sunshine their lives passed on, until the appointed day arrived that was to see them bound, not by the graceful true-lovers' knot, which either might untie, but by a chain light as downy fetters if borne in mutual love, and galling as ponderous iron links, if heart answered not heart and the chafing spirit struggled to get free.

Hartley Emerson loved truly the beautiful, talented and affectionate, but badly-disciplined, quick-tempered, self-willed girl he had chosen for a wife; and Irene Delancy would have gone to prison and to death for the sake of the man to whom she had yielded up the rich treasures of her young heart. In both cases the great drawback to happiness was the absence of self-discipline, self-denial and self-conquest. They could overcome difficulties, brave danger, set the world at defiance, if need be, for each other, and not a coward nerve give way; but when pride and passion came between them, each was a child in weakness and blind self-will. Unfortunately, persistence of character was strong in both. They were of such stuff as martyrs were made of in the fiery times of power and persecution.

A brighter, purer morning than that on which their

marriage vows were said the year had not given to the smiling earth. Clear and softly blue as the eye of childhood bent the summer sky above them. There was not a cloud in all the tranquil heavens to give suggestion of dreary days to come or to wave a sign of warning. The blithe birds sung their matins amid the branches that hung their leafy drapery around and above Irene's windows, in seeming echoes to the songs love was singing in her heart. Nature put on the loveliest attire in all her ample wardrobe, and decked herself with coronals and wreaths of flowers that loaded the air with sweetness.

"May your lives flow together like two pure streams that meet in the same valley, and as bright a sky bend always over you as gives its serene promise for to-day."

Thus spoke the minister as the ceremonials closed that wrought the external bond of union between them. His words were uttered with feeling and solemnity; for marriage, in his eyes, was no light thing. He had seen too many sad hearts struggling in chains that only death could break, ever to regard marriage with other than sober thoughts that went questioning away into the future.

The "amen" of Mr. Delancy was not audibly spoken, but it was deep-voiced in his heart.

There was to be a wedding-tour of a few weeks, and then the young couple were to take possession of a new home in the city, Which Mr. Emerson had prepared for his bride. The earliest boat that came up from New York was to bears the party to Albany, Saratoga being the first point of their destination.

After the closing of the marriage ceremony some two or three hours passed before the time of departure came. The warm congratulations were followed by a gay, festive scene, in which glad young hearts had a merry-making time. How beautiful the bride looked! and how proudly the gaze of her newly-installed husband turned ever and ever toward her, move which way she would among her maidens, as if she were a magnet to his eyes. He was standing in the portico that looked out upon the distant river, about an hour after the wedding, talking with one of the bridesmaids, when the latter, pointing to the sky, said, laughing -

"There comes your fate."

Emerson's eyes followed the direction of her finger.

"You speak in riddles," he replied, looking back into the maiden's face. "What do you see?"

"A little white blemish on the deepening azure," was answered. "There it lies, just over that stately horse-chestnut, whose branches arch themselves into the outline of a great cathedral window."

"A scarcely perceptible cloud?"

"Yes, no bigger than a hand; and just below it is another."

"I see; and yet you still propound a riddle. What has that cloud to do with my fate?"

"You know the old superstition connected with wedding-days?"

"What?"

"That as the aspect of the day is, so will the wedded life be."

"Ours, then, is full of promise. There has been no fairer day than this," said the young man.

"Yet many a day that opened as bright and cloudless has sobbed itself away in tears."

"True; and it may be so again. But I am no believer in signs."

"Nor I," said the young lady, again laughing.

The bride came up at this moment and, hearing the remark of her young husband, said, as she drew her arm within his -

"What about signs, Hartley?"

"Miss Carman has just reminded me of the superstition about wedding-days, as typical of life."

"Oh yes, I remember," said Irene, smiling. "If the day opens clear, then becomes cloudy, and goes out in storm, there will be happiness in the beginning, but sorrow at the close; but if clouds and rain herald its awakening, then pass over and leave the sky blue and sunny, there will be trouble at first, but smiling peace as life progresses and declines. Our sky is bright as heart could wish." And the bride looked up into the deep blue ether.

Miss Carman laid one hand upon her arm and with the

other pointed lower down, almost upon the horizon's edge, saying, in a tone of mock solemnity -

"As I said to Mr. Emerson, so I now say to you - There comes our fate."

"You don't call that the herald of an approaching storm?"

"Weatherwise people say," answered the maiden, "that a sky without a cloud is soon followed by stormy weather. Since morning until now there has not a cloud been seen.'"

"Weatherwise people and almanac-makers speak very oracularly, but the day of auguries and signs is over," replied Irene.

"Philosophy," said Mr. Emerson, "is beginning to find reasons in the nature of things for results that once seemed only accidental, yet followed with remarkable certainty the same phenomena. It discovers a relation of cause and effect where ignorance only recognizes some power working in the dark."

"So you pass me over to the side of ignorance!" Irene spoke in a tone that Hartley's ear recognized too well. His remark had touched her pride.

"Not by any means," he answered quickly, eager to do away the impression. "Not by any means," he repeated. "The day of mere auguries, omens and signs is over. Whatever natural phenomena appear are dependent on natural causes, and men of science are beginning to study the so-called superstitions of farmers and seamen, to find out, if possible, the philosophical elucidation. Already a number of curious results have followed investigation in this field."

Irene leaned on his arm still, but she did not respond. A little cloud had come up and lay just upon the verge of her soul's horizon. Her husband knew that it was there; and this knowledge caused a cloud to dim also the clear azure of his mind. There was a singular correspondence between their mental sky and the fair cerulean without.

Fearing to pursue the theme on which they were conversing, lest some unwitting words might shadow still further the mind of Irene, Emerson changed the subject, and was, to all appearance, successful in dispelling the little cloud.

The hour came, at length, when the bridal party must leave. After a tender, tearful partings with her father, Irene turned her steps away from the home of her childhood into a new path, that would lead her out into the world, where so many thousands upon thousands, who saw only a way of velvet softness before them, have cut their tended feet upon flinty rocks, even to the verve end of their tearful journey. Tightly and long did Mr. Delancy hold his child to his heart, and when his last kiss was given and his fervent "God give you a happy life, my daughter!" said, he gazed after her departing form with eyes front which manly firmness could not hold back the tears.

No one knew better than Mr. Delancy the perils that lay before his daughter. That storms would darken her sky and desolate her heart, he had too good reason to fear. His hope for her lay beyond the summer-time of life, when, chastened by suffering and subdued by experience, a tranquil autumn would crown her soul with blessings that might have been earlier enjoyed. He was not superstitious, and yet it was with a feeling of concern that he saw the white and golden clouds gathering like enchanted land along the horizon, and piling themselves up, one above another, as if in sport, building castles and towers that soon dissolved, changing away into fantastic forms, in which the eye could see no meaning; and when, at last, his ear caught a far-distant sound that jarred the air, a sudden pain shot through his heart.

"On any other day but this!" he sighed to himself, turning from the window at which he was standing and walking restlessly the floor for several minutes, lost in a sad, dreamy reverie.

Like something instinct with life the stately steamer, quivering with every stroke of her iron heart, swept along the gleaming river on her upward passage, bearing to their destination her freight of human souls. Among theme was our bridal party, which, as the day was so clear and beautiful, was gathered upon the upper deck. As Irene's eyes turned from the closing vision of her father's beautiful home, where the first cycle of her life had recorded its golden hours, she said, with a sigh, speaking to one of her companions -

"Farewell, Ivy Cliff! I shall return to you again, but not the same being I was when I left your pleasant scenes this morning."

"A happier being I trust," replied Miss Carman, one of her bridemaids.

Rose Carman was a young friend , residing in the

neighborhood of her father, to whom Irene was tenderly attached.

"Something here says no." And Irene, bending toward Miss Carman, pressed one of her hands against her bosom.

"The weakness of an hour like this," answered her friend with an assuring smile. "It will pass away like the morning cloud and the early dew."

Mr. Emerson noticed the shade upon the face of his bride, and drawing near to her, said, tenderly -

"I can forgive you a sigh for the past, Irene. Ivy Cliff is a lovely spot, and your home has been all that a maiden's heart could desire. It would be strange, indeed, if the chords that have so long bound you there did not pull at your heart in parting."

Irene did not answer, but let her eyes turn backward with a pensive almost longing glance toward the spot where lay hidden among the distant trees the home of her early years. A deep shadow had suddenly fallen upon her spirits. Whence it came she knew not and asked not; but with the shadow was a dim foreboding of evil.

There was tact and delicacy enough in the companions of Irene to lead them to withdraw observation and to withhold further remarks until she could recover the self-possession she had lost. This came back in a little while, when, with an effort, she put on the light, easy manner so natural to her.

"Looking at the signs?" said one of the party, half an

hour afterward, as she saw the eyes of Irene ranging along the sky, where clouds were now seen towering up in steep masses, like distant mountains.

"If I were a believer of signs," replied Irene, placing her arm within that of the maiden who had addressed her, and drawing her partly aside, "I might feel sober at this portent. But I am not. Still, sign or no sign, I trust we are not going to have a storm. It would greatly mar our pleasure."

But long ere the boat reached Albany, rain began to fall, accompanied by lightning and thunder; and soon the clouds were dissolving in a mimic deluge. Hour after hour, the wind and rain and lightning held fierce revelry, and not until near the completion of the voyage did the clouds hold back their watery treasures, and the sunbeams force themselves through the storm's dark barriers,

When the stars came out that evening, studding the heavens with light, there was no obscuring spot on all the o'erarching sky.

CHAPTER IV.

UNDER THE CLOUD.

THE wedding party was to spend a week at Saratoga, and it was now the third day since its arrival. The time had passed pleasantly, or wearily, according to the state of mind or social habits and resources of the individual. The bride, it was remarked by some of the party, seemed dull; and Rose Carman, who knew her friend better, perhaps, than any other individual in the company, and kept her under close observation, was concerned to notice an occasional curtness of manner toward her husband, that was evidently not relished. Something had already transpired to jar the chords so lately attuned to harmony.

After dinner a ride was proposed by one of the company. Emerson responded favorably, but Irene was indifferent. He urged her, and she gave an evidently reluctant consent. While the gentlemen went to make arrangement for carriages, the ladies retired to their rooms. Miss Carman accompanied the bride. She had noticed her manner, and felt slightly troubled at her state of mind, knowing, as she did, her impulsive character and blind self-will when excited by opposition.

" I don't want to ride to-day ! " exclaimed Irene,

throwing herself into a chair as soon as she had entered her room; "and Hartley knows that I do not."

Her cheeks burned and her eyes sparkled.

"If it will give him pleasure to ride out," said Rose, in a gentle soothing manner, "you cannot but have the same feeling in accompanying him."

"I beg your pardon!" replied Irene, briskly. "If I don't want to ride, no company can make the act agreeable. Why can't people learn to leave others in freedom? If Hartley had shown the same unwillingness to join this riding party that I manifested, do you think I would have uttered a second word in favor of going? No. I am provoked at his persistence."

"There, there, Irene!" said Miss Carman, drawing an arm tenderly around the neck of her friend; "don't trust such sentences on your lips. I can't bear to hear you talk so. It isn't my sweet friend speaking."

"You are a dear, good girl, Rose," replied Irene, smiling faintly, "and I only wish that I had a portion of your calm, gentle spirit. But I am as I am, and must act out if I act at all. I must be myself or nothing."

"You can be as considerate of others as of yourself?" said Rose.

Irene looked at her companion inquiringly.

"I mean," added Rose, "that you can exercise the virtue of self-denial in order to give pleasure to another - especially if that other one be an object very dear to you. As in the present case, seeing that your husband wants to join this riding party, you can, for his sake, lay aside your indifference, and enter, with a hearty good-will, into the proposed pastime."

"And why cannot he, seeing that I do not care to ride, deny himself a little for my sake, and not drag me out against my will? Is all the yielding and concession to be on my side? Must his will rule in everything? I can tell you what it is, Rose, this will never suit me. There will be open war between us before the honeymoon has waxed and waned, if he goes on as he has begun."

"Hush! hush, Irene!" said her friend, in a tone of deprecation. "The lightest sense of wrong gains undue magnitude the moment we begin to complain. We see almost anything to be of greater importance when from the obscurity of thought we bring it out into the daylight of speech."

"It will be just as I say, and saying it will not make it any more so," was Irene's almost sullen response to this. "I have my own ideas of things and my own individuality, and neither of these do I mean to abandon. If Hartley hasn't the good sense to let me have my own way in what concerns myself, I will take my own way. As to the troubles that may come afterward, I do not give them any weight in the argument. I would die a martyr's deaths rather than become the passive creature of another."

"My dear friend, why will you talk so?" Rose spoke in a tone of grief.

"Simply because I am in earnest. From the hour of our marriage I have seen a disposition on the part of my husband to assume control - to make his will the general law of our actions. It has not exhibited itself in things of moment, but in trifles, showing that the spirit was there. I say this to you, Rose, because we have been like sisters, and I can tell you of my inmost thoughts. There is a cloud already in the sky, and it threatens an approaching storm."

"Oh, my friend, why are you so blind, so weak, so self-deceived? You are putting forth your hands to drag down the temple of happiness. If it fall, it will crush you beneath a mass of ruins; and not you only, but the one you have so lately pledged yourself before God and his angels to love."

"And I do love him as deeply as ever man was loved. Oh that he knew my heart! He would not then shatter his image there. He would not trifle with a spirit formed for intense, yielding, passionate love, but rigid as steel and cold as ice when its freedom is touched. He should have known me better before linking his fate with mine."

One of her darker moods had come upon Irene, and she was beating about in the blind obscurity of passion. As she began to give utterance to complaining thoughts, new thoughts formed themselves, and what was only vague feelings grew into ideas of wrong; and these, when once spoken, assumed a magnitude unimagined before. In vain did her friend strive with her. Argument, remonstrance, persuasion, only seemed to bring greater obscurity and to excite a more bitter feeling in her mind. And so, despairing of any good result, Rose withdrew, and left her with her own unhappy thoughts.

Not long after Miss Carman retired, Emerson came in.

At the sound of his approaching footsteps, Irene had, with a strong effort, composed herself and swept back the deeper shadows from her face.

"Not ready yet?" he said, in a pleasant, half-chiding way. "The carriages will be at the door in ten minutes."

"I am not going to ride out," returned Irene, in a quiet, seemingly indifferent tone of voice. Hartley mistook her manner for sport, and answered pleasantly -

"Oh yes you are, my little lady."

"No, I am not." There was no misapprehension now.

"Not going to ride out?" Hartley's brows contracted.

"No; I am not going to ride out to-day." Each word was distinctly spoken.

"I don't understand you, Irene."

"Are not my words plain enough?"

"Yes, they are too plain - so plain as to make them involve a mystery. What do you mean by this sudden change of purpose?"

"I don't wish to ride out," said Irene, with assumed calmness of manner; "and that being so, may I not have my will in the case?"

"No -"

A red spot burned on Irene's cheeks and her eyes flashed.

T. S. Arthur

"No," repeated her husband; "not after you have given up that will to another."

"To you!" Irene started to her feet in instant passion. "And so I am to be nobody, and you the lord and master. My will is to be nothing, and yours the law of my life." Her lip curled in contemptuous anger.

"You misunderstand me," said Hartley Emerson, speaking as calmly as was possible in this sudden emergency. "I did not refer specially to myself, but to all of our party, to whom you had given up your will in a promise to ride out with them, and to whom, therefore, you were bound."

"An easy evasion," retorted the excited bride, who had lost her mental equipoise.

"Irene," the young man spoke sternly, "are those the right words for your husband? An easy evasion!"

"I have said them."

"And you must unsay them."

Both had passed under the cloud which pride and passion had raised.

"Must! I thought you knew me better, Hartley." Irene grew suddenly calm.

"If there is to be love between us, all barriers must be removed."

"Don't say *must* to me, sir! I will not endure the word."

Hartley turned from her and walked the floor with rapid steps, angry, grieved and in doubt as to what it were best for him to do. The storm had broken on him without a sign of warning, and he was wholly unprepared to meet it.

"Irene," he said, at length, pausing before her, "this conduct on your part is wholly inexplicable. I cannot understand its meaning. Will you explain yourself?"

"Certainly. I am always ready to give a reason for my conduct," she replied, with cold dignity.

"Say on, then." Emerson spoke with equal coldness of manner.

"I did not wish to ride out, and said so in the beginning. That ought to have been enough for you. But no - my wishes were nothing; your will must be law."

"And that is all! the head and front of my offending!" said Emerson, in a tone of surprise.

"It isn't so much the thing itself that I object to, as the spirit in which it is done," said Irene.

"A spirit of overbearing self-will!' said Emerson.

"Yes, if you choose. That is what my soul revolts against. I gave you my heart and my hand - my love and my confidence - not my freedom. The last is a part of my being, and I will maintain it while I have life."

"Perverse girl! What insane spirit has got possession of

your mind?" exclaimed Emerson, chafed beyond endurance.

"Say on," retorted Irene; "I am prepared for this. I have seen, from the hour of our marriage, that a time of strife would come; that your will would seek to make itself ruler, and that I would not submit. I did not expect the issue to come so soon. I trusted in your love to spare me, at least, until I could be bidden from general observation when I turned myself upon you and said, Thus far thou mayest go, but no farther. But, come the struggle early or late - now or in twenty years - I am prepared."

There came at this moment a rap at their door. Mr. Emerson opened it.

"Carriage is waiting," said a servant.

"Say that we will be down in a few minutes."

The door closed.

"Come, Irene," said Mr. Emerson.

"You spoke very confidently to the servant, and said we would be down in a few minutes."

"There, there, Irene! Let this folly die; it has lived long enough. Come! Make yourself ready with all speed - our party is delayed by this prolonged absence."

"You think me trifling, and treat me as if I were a captious child," said Irene, with chilling calmness; "but I am neither."

"Then you will not go?"

"I will not go." She said the words slowly and deliberately, and as she spoke looked her husband steadily in the face. She was in earnest, and he felt that further remonstrance would be in vain.

"You will repent of this," he replied, with enough of menace in his voice to convey to her mind a great deal more than was in his thoughts. And he turned from her and left the room. Going down stairs, he found the riding-party waiting for their appearance.

"Where is Irene?" was asked by one and another, on seeing him alone.

"She does not care to ride out this afternoon, and so I have excused her," he replied. Miss Carman looked at him narrowly, and saw that there was a shade of trouble on his countenance, which he could not wholly conceal. She would have remained behind with Irene, but that would have disappointed the friend who was to be her companion in the drive.

As the party was in couples, and as Mr. Emerson had made up his mind to go without his young wife, he had to ride alone. The absence of Irene was felt as a drawback to the pleasure of all the company. Miss Carman, who understood the real cause of Irene's refusal to ride, was so much troubled in her mind that she sat almost silent during the two hours they were out. Mr. Emerson left the party after they had been out for an hour, and returned to the hotel. His excitement had cooled off, and he began to feel regret at the unbending way in which he had met his bride's unhappy mood.

"Her over-sensitive mind has taken up a wrong impression," he said, as he talked with himself; "and, instead of saying or doing anything to increase that impression, I should, by word and act of kindness, have done all in my power for its removal. Two wrongs never make a right. Passion met by passion results not in peace. I should have soothed and yielded, and so won her back to reason. As a man, I ought to possess a cooler and more rationally balanced mind. She is a being of feeling and impulse, - loving, ardent, proud, sensitive and strong-willed. Knowing this, it was madness in me to chafe instead of soothing her; to oppose, when gentle concession would have torn from her eyes an illusive veil. Oh that I could learn wisdom in time! I was in no ignorance as to her peculiar character. I knew her faults and her weaknesses, as well as her nobler qualities; and it was for me to stimulate the one and bear with the others. Duty, love, honor, humanity, all pointed to this."

The longer Mr. Emerson's thoughts ran in this direction, the deeper grew his feeling of self-condemnation, and the more tenderly yearned his heart toward the young creature he had left alone with the enemies of their peace nestling in her bosom and filling it with passion and pain. After separating himself from his party, he drove back toward the hotel at a speed that soon put his horses into a foam.

CHAPTER V.

THE BURSTING OF THE STORM.

MR. DELANCY was sitting in his library on the afternoon of the fourth day since the wedding-party left Ivy Cliff, when the entrance of some one caused him to turn toward the door.

"Irene!" he exclaimed, in a tone of anxiety and alarm, as he started to his feet; for his daughter stood before him. Her face was pale, her eyes fixed and sad, her dress in disorder.

"Irene, in Heaven's name, what has happened?"

"The worst," she answered, in a low, hoarse voice, not moving from the spot where she first stood still.

"Speak plainly, my child. I cannot bear suspense."

"I have left my husband and returned to you!" was the firmly uttered reply.

"Oh, folly! oh, madness! What evil counselor has prevailed with you, my unhappy child?" said Mr. Delancy, in a voice of anguish.

"I have counseled with no one but myself."

T. S. Arthur

"Never a wise counselor - never a wise counselor! But why, why have you taken this desperate step?"

"In self-protection," replied Irene.

"Sit down, my child. There!" and he led her to a seat. "Now let me remove your bonnet and shawl. How wretched you look, poor, misguided one! I could have laid you in the grave with less agony than I feel in seeing you thus."

Her heart was touched at this, and tears fell over her face. In the selfishness of her own sternly-borne trouble, she had forgotten the sorrow she was bringing to her father's heart.

"Poor child! poor child!" sobbed the old man, as he sat down beside Irene and drew her head against his breast. And so both wept together for a time. After they had grown calm, Mr. Delancy said -

"Tell me, Irene, without disguise of any kind, the meaning of this step which you have so hastily taken. Let me have the beginning, progress and consummation of the sad misunderstanding."

While yet under the government of blind passion, ere her husband returned from the drive which Irene had refused to take with him, she had, acting from a sudden suggestion that came to her mind, left her room and, taking the cars, passed down to Albany, where she remained until morning at one of the hotels. In silence and loneliness she had, during the almost sleepless night that followed, ample time for reflection and repentance. And both came, with convictions of error and deep regret for the unwise, almost disgraceful step she had taken, involving not only suffering, but humiliating exposure of herself and husband. But it was felt to be too late now to look back. Pride would have laid upon her a positive interdiction, if other considerations had not come in to push the question of return aside.

In the morning, without partaking of food, Irene left in the New York boat, and passed down the river toward the home from which she had gone forth, only a few days before, a happy bride - returning with the cup, then full of the sweet wine of life, now brimming with the bitterest potion that had ever touched her lips.

And so she had come back to her father's house. In all the hours of mental anguish which had passed since her departure from Saratoga, there had been an accusing spirit at her ear, and, resist as she would, self-condemnation prevailed over attempted self-justification. The cause of this unhappy rupture was so slight, the first provocation so insignificant, that she felt the difficulty of making out her case before her father. As to the world, pride counseled silence.

With but little concealment or extenuation of her own conduct, Irene told the story of her disagreement with Hartley.

"And that was all!" exclaimed Mr. (sic) Delancey, in amazement, when she ended her narrative.

"All, but enough!" she answered, with a resolute manner.

Mr. Delancy arose and walked the floor in silence for more than ten minutes, during which time Irene neither spoke nor moved.

"Oh, misery!" ejaculated the father, at length, lifting his hands above his head and then bringing them down with a gesture of despair.

Irene started up and moved to his side.

"Dear father!" She spoke tenderly, laying her hands upon him; but he pushed her away, saying -

"Wretched girl! you have laid upon my old head a burden of disgrace and wretchedness that you have no power to remove."

"Father! father!" She clung to him, but he pushed her away. His manner was like that of one suddenly bereft of reason. She clung still, but he resolutely tore himself from her, when she fell exhausted and fainting upon the floor.

Alarm now took the place of other emotions, and Mr. Delancy was endeavoring to lift the insensible body, when a quick, heavy tread in the portico caused him to look up, just as Hartley Emerson pushed open one of the French windows and entered the library. He had a wild, anxious, half-frightened look. Mr. Delancy let the body fall from his almost paralyzed arms and staggered to a chair, while Emerson sprung forward, catching up the fainting form of his young bride and bearing it to a sofa.

"How long has she been in this way?" asked the young man, in a tone of agitation.

"She fainted this moment," replied Mr. Delancy.

"How long has she been here?"

"Not half an hour," was answered; and as Mr. Delancy spoke he reached for the bell and jerked it two or three times violently. The waiter, startled by the loud, prolonged sound, came hurriedly to the library.

"Send Margaret here, and then get a horse and ride over swiftly for Dr. Edmundson. Tell him to come immediately."

The waiter stood for a moment or two, looking in a half-terrified way upon the white, deathly face of Irene, and then fled from the apartment. No grass grew beneath his horse's feet as he held him to his utmost speed for the distance of two miles, which lay between Ivy Cliff and the doctor's residence.

Margaret, startled by the hurried, half-incoherent summons of the waiter, came flying into the library. The moment her eyes rested upon Irene, who still insensible upon the sofa, she screamed out, in terror -

"Oh, she's dead! she's dead!" and stood still as if suddenly paralyzed; then, wringing her hands, she broke out in a wild, sobbing tone -

"My poor, poor child! Oh, she is dead, dead!"

"No, Margaret," said Mr. Delancy, as calmly as he could speak, "she is not dead; it is only a fainting fit. Bring some water, quickly."

Water was brought and dashed into the face of Irene; but there came no sign of returning consciousness.

"Hadn't you better take her up to her room, Mr. Emerson?" suggested Margaret.

"Yes," he replied; and, lifting the insensible form of his bride in his arms, the unhappy man bore her to her chamber. Then, sitting down beside the bed upon which he had placed her, he kissed her pale cheeks and, laying his face to hers, sobbed and moaned, in the abandonment of his grief, like a distressed child weeping in despair for some lost treasure.

"Come," said Margaret, who was an old family domestic, drawing Hartley from the bedside, "leave her alone with me for a little while."

And the husband and father retired from the room. When they returned, at the call of Margaret, they found Irene in bed, her white, unconscious face scarcely relieved against the snowy pillow on which her head was resting.

"She is alive," said Margaret, in a low and excited voice; "I can feel her heart beat."

"Thank God!" ejaculated Emerson, bending again over the motionless form and gazing anxiously down upon the face of his bride.

But there was no utterance of thankfulness in the heart of Mr. Delancy. For her to come back again to conscious life was, he felt, but a return to wretchedness. If the true prayer of his heart could have found voice, it would have been for death, and not for life.

In silence, fear and suspense they waited an hour before the doctor arrived. Little change in Irene took place during that time, except that her respiration became clearer and the pulsations of her heart distinct and regular. The application of warm stimulants was immediately ordered, and their good effects soon became apparent.

"All will come right in a little while," said Dr. Edmundson, encouragingly. "It seems to be only a fainting fit of unusual length."

Hartley drew Mr. Delancy aside.

"It will be best that I should be alone with her when she recovers," said he.

"You may be right in that," said Mr. Delancy, after a moment's reflection.

"I am sure that I am," was returned.

"You think she will recover soon?" said Mr. Delancy, approaching the doctor.

"Yes, at any moment. She is breathing deeper, and her heart beats with a fuller impulse."

"Let us, retire, then;" and he drew the doctor from the apartment. Pausing at the door, he called to Margaret in a half whisper. She went out also, Emerson alone remaining.

Taking his place by the bedside, he waited, in trembling anxiety, for the moment when her eyes should open and recognize him. At last there came a quivering of the eyelids and a motion about the sleeper's lips. Emerson bent over and took one of her hands in his.

"Irene!" He called her name in a voice of the tenderest affection. The sound seemed to penetrate to the region of consciousness, for her lips moved with a murmur of inarticulate words. He kissed her, and said again -

"Irene!"

There was a sudden lighting up of her face.

"Irene, love! darling!" The voice of Emerson was burdened with tenderness.

"Oh, Hartley!" she exclaimed, opening her eyes and looking with a kind of glad bewilderment into his face. Then, half rising and drawing her arms around his neck, she hid her face on his bosom, murmuring -

"Thank God that it is only a dream!"

"Yes, thank God!" replied her husband, as he kissed her in a kind of wild fervor; "and may such dreams never come again."

She lay very still for some moments. Thought and memory were beginning to act feebly. The response of her husband had in it something that set her to questioning. But there was one thing that made her feel happy: the sound of his loving voice was in her ears; and all the while she felt his hand moving, with a soft, caressing touch, over her cheek and temple.

"Dear Irene!" he murmured in her ears; and then her hand tightened on his.

And thus she remained until conscious life regained its full activity. Then the trial came.

Suddenly lifting herself from the bosom of her husband, Irene gave a hurried glance around the well-known chamber, then turned and looked with a strange, fearful questioning glance into his face:

"Where am I? What does this mean?"

"It means," replied Emerson, "that the dream, thank God! is over, and that my dear wife is awake again."

He placed his arms again around her and drew her to his heart, almost smothering her, as he did so, with kisses.

She lay passive for a little while; then, disengaging herself, she said, faintly -

"I feel weak and bewildered; let me lie down."

She closed her eyes as Emerson placed her back on the pillow, a sad expression covering her still pallid face. Sitting down beside her, he took her hand and held it with a firm pressure. She did not attempt to withdraw it. He kissed her, and a warmer flush came over her face.

"Dear Irene!" His hand pressed tightly upon hers, and she returned the pressure.

"Shall I call your father? He is very anxious about you."

" Not yet. " And she caught slightly her breath, as if

feeling were growing too strong for her.

"Let it be as a dream, Hartley." Irene lifted herself up and looked calmly, but with a very sad expression on her countenance, into her husband's face.

"Between us two, Irene, even as a dream from which both have awakened," he replied.

She closed her eyes and sunk back upon the pillow.

Mr. Emerson then went to the door and spoke to Mr. Delancy. On a brief consultation it was thought best for Dr. Edmundson not to see her again. A knowledge of the fact that he had been called in might give occasion for more disturbing thoughts than were already pressing upon her mind. And so, after giving some general directions as to the avoidance of all things likely to excite her mind unpleasantly, the doctor withdrew.

Mr. Delancy saw his daughter alone. The interview was long and earnest. On his part was the fullest disapproval of her conduct and the most solemnly spoken admonitions and warnings. She confessed her error, without any attempt at excuse or palliation, and promised a wiser conduct in the future.

"There is not one husband in five," said the father, "who would have forgiven an act like this, placing him, as it does, in such a false and humiliating position before the world. He loves you with too deep and true a love, my child, for girlish trifling like this. And let me warn you of the danger you incur of turning against you the spirit of such a man. I have studied his character closely, and I see in it an element of firmness that, if it once sets itself, will be as inflexible as iron. If you repeat acts of this kind, the day must come when forbearance will cease; and then, in turning from you, it will be never to turn back again. Harden him against you once, and it will be for all time."

Irene wept bitterly at this strong representation, and trembled at thought of the danger she had escaped.

To her husband, when she was alone with him again, she confessed her fault, and prayed him to let the memory of it pass from his mind for ever. On his part was the fullest denial of any purpose whatever, in the late misunderstanding, to bend her to his will. He assured her that if he had dreamed of any serious objection on her part to the ride, he would not have urged it for a moment. It involved no promised pleasure to him apart from pleasure to her; and it was because he believed that she would enjoy the drive that he had urged her to make one of the party.

All this was well, as far as it could go. But repentance and mutual forgiveness did not restore everything to the old condition - did not obliterate that one sad page in their history, and leave them free to make a new and better record. If the folly had been in private, the effort at forgiving and forgetting would have been attended with fewer annoying considerations. But it was committed in public, and under circumstances calculated to attract attention and occasion invidious remark. And then, how were they to meet the different members of the wedding-party, which they had so suddenly thrown into consternation?

On the next day the anxious members of this party made their appearance at Ivy Cliff, not having, up to this time, received any intelligence of the fugitive bride. Mr. Delancy did not attempt to excuse to them the unjustifiable conduct of his daughter, beyond the admission that she must have been temporarily deranged. Something was said about resuming the bridal tour, but Mr. Delancy said, "No; the quiet of Ivy Cliff will yield more pleasure than the excitement of travel."

And all felt this to be true.

CHAPTER VI.

AFTER THE STORM.

AFTER the storm. Alas! that there should be a wreck-strewn shore so soon! That within three days of the bridal morning a tempest should have raged, scattering on the wind sweet blossoms which had just opened to the sunshine, tearing away the clinging vines of love, and leaving marks of desolation which no dew and sunshine could ever obliterate!

It was not a blessed honeymoon to them. How could it be, after what had passed? Both were hurt and mortified; and while there was mutual forgiveness and great tenderness and fond concessions, one toward the other, there was a sober, (sic) thoughful state of mind, not favorable to happiness.

Mr. Delancy hoped the lesson - a very severe one - might prove the guarantee of future peace. It had, without doubt, awakened Irene's mind to sober thoughts - and closer self-examination than usual. She was convicted in her own heart of folly, the memory of which could never return to her without a sense of pain.

At the end of three weeks from the day of their marriage, Mr. And Mrs. Emerson went down to the

T. S. Arthur

city to take possession of their new home. On the eve of their departure from Ivy Cliff, Mr. Delancy had a long conference with his daughter, in which he conjured her, by all things sacred, to guard herself against that blindness of passion which had already produced such unhappy consequences. She repeated, with many tears, her good resolutions for the future, and showed great sorrow and contrition for the past.

"It may come out right," said the old man to himself; as he sat alone, with a pressure of foreboding on his mind, looking into the dim future, on the day of their departure for New York. His only and beloved child had gone forth to return no more, unless in sorrow or wretchedness. "It may come out right, but my heart has sad misgivings."

There was a troubled suspense of nearly a week, when the first letter came from Irene to her father. He broke the seal with unsteady hands, fearing to let his eyes fall upon the opening page.

"My dear, dear father! I am a happy young wife."

"Thank God!" exclaimed the old man aloud, letting the hand fall that held Irene's letter. It was some moments before he could read farther; then he drank in, with almost childish eagerness, every sentence of the long letter.

"Yes, yes, it may come out right," said Mr. Delancy; "it may come out right." He uttered the words, so often on his lips, with more confidence than usual. The letter strongly urged him to make her a visit, if it was only for a day or two.

"You know, dear father," she wrote, "that most of your time is to be spent with us - all your winters, certainly; and we want you to begin the new arrangement as soon as possible."

Mr. Delancy sighed over the passage. He had not set his heart on this arrangement. It might have been a pleasant thing for him to anticipate; but there was not the hopeful basis for anticipation which a mind like his required.

Not love alone prompted Mr. Delancy to make an early visit to New York; a feeling of anxiety to know how it really was with the young couple acted quite as strongly in the line of incentive. And so he went down to the city and passed nearly a week there. Both Irene and her husband knew that he was observing them closely all the while, and a consciousness of this put them under some constraint. Everything passed harmoniously, and Mr. Delancy returned with the half-hopeful, half-doubting words on his lips, so often and often repeated -

"Yes, yes, it may come out right."

But it was not coming out altogether right. Even while the old man was under her roof, Irene had a brief season of self-willed reaction against her husband, consequent on some unguarded word or act, which she felt to be a trespass on her freedom. To save appearances while Mr. Delancy was with them, Hartley yielded and tendered conciliation, all the while that his spirit chafed sorely.

The departure of Mr. Delancy for Ivy Cliff was the signal for both Irene and her husband to lay aside a portion of the restraint which each had borne with a certain restlessness that longed for a time of freedom. On the very day that he left Irene showed so much that seemed to her husband like perverseness of will that he was seriously offended, and spoke an unguarded word that was as fire to stubble - a word that was repented of as soon as spoken, but which pride would not permit him to recall. It took nearly a week of suffering to discipline the mind of Mr. Emerson to the point of conciliation. On the part of Irene there was not the thought of yielding. Her will, supported by pride, was as rigid as iron. Reason had no power over her. She felt, rather than thought.

Thus far, both as lover and husband, in all their alienations, Hartley had been the first to yield; and it was so now. He was strong-willed and persistent; but cooler reason helped him back into the right way, and he had, thus far, found it quicker than Irene. Not that he suffered less or repented sooner. Irene's suffering was far deeper, but she was blinder and more self-determined.

Again the sun of peace smiled down upon them, but, as before, on something shorn of its strength or beauty.

"I will be more guarded," said Hartley to himself. "Knowing her weakness, why should I not protect her against everything that wounds her sensitive nature? Love concedes, is long suffering and full of patience. I love Irene - words cannot tell how deeply. Then why should I not, for her sake, bear and forbear? Why should I think of myself and grow fretted because she does not yield as readily as I could desire to my wishes?"

So Emerson talked with himself and resolved. But who does not know the feebleness of resolution when opposed to temperament and confirmed habits of mind? How weak is mere human strength! Alas! How few, depending on that alone, are ever able to bear up steadily, for any length of time, against the tide of passion!

Off his guard in less than twenty-four hours after resolving thus with himself, the young husband spoke in captious disapproval of something which Irene had done or proposed to do, and the consequence was the assumption on her part of a cold, reserved and dignified manner, which hurt and annoyed him beyond measure. Pride led him to treat her in the same way; and so for days they met in silence or formal courtesy, all the while suffering a degree of wretchedness almost impossible to be endured, and all the while, which was worst of all, writing on their hearts bitter things against each other.

To Emerson, as before, the better state first returned, and the sunshine of his countenance drove the shadows from hers. Then for a season they were loving, thoughtful, forbearing and happy. But the clouds came back again, and storms marred the beauty of their lives.

All this was sad - very sad. There were good and noble qualities in the hearts of both. They were not narrow-minded and selfish, like so many of your placid, accommodating, calculating people, but generous in their feelings and broad in their sympathies. They had ideals of life that went reaching out far beyond themselves. Yes, it was sad to see two such hearts beating against and bruising each other, instead of taking the same pulsation. But there seemed to be no

T. S. Arthur

help for them. Irene's jealous guardianship of her freedom, her quick temper, pride and self-will made the position of her husband so difficult that it was almost impossible for him to avoid giving offence.

The summer and fall passed away without any serious rupture between the sensitive couple, although there had been seasons of great unhappiness to both. Irene had been up to Ivy Cliff many times to visit her father, and now she was, beginning to urge his removal to the city for the winter; but Mr. Delancy, who had never given his full promise to this arrangement, felt less and less inclined to leave his old home as the season advanced. Almost from boyhood he had lived there, and his habits were formed for rural instead of city life.

He pictured the close streets, with their rows of houses, that left for the eye only narrow patches of ethereal blue, and contrasted this with the broad winter landscape, which for him had always spread itself out with a beauty rivaled by no other season, and his heart failed him.

The brief December days were on them, and Irene grew more urgent.

"Come, dear father," she wrote. "I think of you, sitting all alone at Ivy Cliff, during these long evenings, and grow sad at heart in sympathy with your loneliness. Come at once. Why linger a week or even a day longer? We have been all in all to each other these many years, and ought not to be separated now."

But Mr. Delancy was not ready to exchange the pure air and widespreading scenery of the Highlands for a city residence, even in the desolate winter, and so wrote back doubtingly. Irene and her husband then came up to add the persuasion of their presence at Ivy Cliff. It did not avail, however. The old man was too deeply wedded to his home.

"I should be miserable in New York," he replied to their earnest entreaties; "and it would not add to your happiness to see me going about with a sober, discontented face, or to be reminded every little while that if you had left me to my winter's hibernation I would have been a contented instead of a dissatisfied old man. No, no, my children; Ivy Cliff is the best place for me. You shall come up and spend Christmas here, and we will have a gay season."

There was no further use in argument. Mr. Delancy would have his way; and he was right.

Irene and her husband went back to the city, with a promise to spend Christmas at the old homestead.

Two weeks passed. It was the twentieth of December. Without previous intimation, Irene came up alone to Ivy Cliff, startling her father by coming in suddenly upon him one dreary afternoon, just as the leaden sky began to scatter down the winter's first offering of snow.

"My daughter!" he exclaimed, so surprised that he could not move from where he was sitting.

"Dear father!" she answered with a loving smile, throwing her arms around his neck and kissing him.

"Where is Hartley?" asked the old man, looking past Irene toward the door through which she had just entered.

"Oh, I left him in New York," she replied.

"In New York! Have you come alone?"

"Yes. Christmas is only five days off, you know, and I am here to help you prepare for it. Of course, Hartley cannot leave his business."

She spoke in an excited, almost gay tone of voice. Mr. Delancy looked at her earnestly. Unpleasant doubts flitted through his mind.

"When will your husband come up?" he inquired.

"At Christmas," she answered, without hesitation.

"Why didn't you write, love?" asked Mr. Delancy. "You have taken me by surprise, and set my nerves in a flutter."

"I only thought about it last evening. One of my sudden resolutions."

And she laughed a low, fluttering laugh. It might have been an error, but her father had a fancy that it did not come from her heart.

"I will run up stairs and put off my things," she said, moving away.

"Did you bring a trunk?"

"Oh yes; it is at the landing. Will you send for it?"

And Irene went, with quick steps, from the apartment, and ran up to the chamber she still called her own. On the way she met Margaret.

"Miss Irene!" exclaimed the latter, pausing and lifting her hands in astonishment. "Why, where did you come from?"

"Just arrived in the boat. Have come to help you get ready for Christmas."

"Please goodness, how you frightened me!" said the warm-hearted domestic, who had been in the family ever since Irene was a child, and was strongly attached to her. "How's Mr. Emerson?"

"Oh, he's well, thank you, Margaret."

"Well now, child, you did set me all into a fluster. I thought maybe you'd got into one of your tantrums, and come off and left your husband."

"Why, Margaret!" A crimson flush mantled the face of Irene.

"You must excuse me, child, but just that came into my head," replied Margaret. "You're very downright and determined sometimes; and there isn't anything hardly that you wouldn't do if the spirit was on you. I'm glad it's all right. Dear me! dear me!"

"Oh, I'm not quite so bad as you all make me out," said Irene, laughing.

"I don't think you are bad," answered Margaret, in kind deprecation, yet with a freedom of speech warranted by her years and attachment to Irene. "But you go off in such strange ways - get so wrong-headed sometimes - that there's no counting on you."

Then, growing more serious, she added -

"The fact is, Miss Irene, you keep me feeling kind of uneasy all the time. I dreamed about you last night, and maybe that has helped to put me into a fluster now."

"Dreamed about me!" said Irene, with a degree of interest in her manner.

"Yes. But don't stand here, Miss Irene; come over to your room."

"What kind of a dream had you, Margaret?" asked the young wife, as she sat down on the side of the bed where, pillowed in sleep, she had dreamed so many of girlhood's pleasant dreams.

"I was dreaming all night about you," replied Margaret, looking sober-faced.

"And you saw me in trouble?"

"Oh dear, yes; in nothing but trouble. I thought once that I saw you in a great room full of wild beasts. They were chained or in cages; but you would keep going close up to the bars of the cages, or near enough for the chained animals to spring upon you. And that wasn't all. You put the end of your little parasol in between the bars, and a fierce tiger struck at you with his great cat-like paw, tearing the flesh from your arm. Then I saw you in a little boat, down on the river. You had put up a sail, and was going out all alone. I saw the boat move off from the shore just as plainly as I see you now. I stood and watched until you were in the middle of the river. Then I thought Mr. Emerson was standing by me, and that we both saw a great monster - a whale, or something else - chasing after your boat. Mr. Emerson was in great distress, and said, 'I told her not to go, but she is so self-willed.' And then he jumped into a boat and, taking the oars, went gliding out after you as swiftly as the wind. I never saw mortal arm make a boat fly as he did that little skiff. And I saw him strike the monster with his oar just as his huge jaws were opened to devour you. Dear! dear; but I was frightened, and woke up all in a tremble."

"Before he had saved me?" said Irene, taking a deep breath.

"Yes; but I don't think there was any chance of saving there, and I was glad that I waked up when I did."

"What else did you dream?" asked Irene.

"Oh, I can't tell you all I dreamed. Once I saw you fall from the high rock just above West Point and go dashing down into the river. Then I saw you chased by a mad bull."

"And no one came to my rescue?"

"Oh yes, there was more than one who tried to save you. First, your father ran in between you and the bull; but he dashed over him. Then I saw Mr. Emerson rushing up with a pitchfork, and he got before the mad animal and pointed the sharp prongs at his eyes; but the bull tore down on him and tossed him away up into the air. I awoke as I saw him falling on the sharp-pointed horns that were held up to catch him."

"Well, Margaret, you certainly had a night of horrors," said Irene, in a sober way.

"Indeed, miss, and I had; such a night as I don't wish to have again."

"And your dreaming was all about me?"

"Yes."

"And I was always in trouble or danger?"

"Yes, always; and it was mostly your own fault, too. And that reminds me of what the minister told us in his sermon last Sunday. He said that there were a great many kinds of trouble in this world - some coming from the outside and some coming from the inside; that the outside troubles, which we couldn't help, were generally easiest to be borne; while the inside troubles, which we might have prevented, were the bitterest things in life, because there was remorse as well as suffering. I understood very well what he meant."

"I am afraid," said Irene, speaking partly to herself, "that most of my troubles come from the inside."

"I'm afraid they do," spoke out the frank domestic.

"Margaret!"

"Indeed, miss, and I do think so. If you'd only get right here" - laying her hand upon her breast - "somebody beside yourself would be a great deal happier. There now, child, I've said it; and you needn't go to getting angry with me."

"They are often our best friends who use the plainest speech," said Irene. "No, Margaret, I am not going to be angry with one whom I know to be true-hearted."

"Not truer-hearted than your husband, Miss Irene; nor half so loving."

"Why did you say that?" Margaret started at the tone of voice in which this interrogation was made.

"Because I think so," she answered naively.

Irene looked at her for some moments with a penetrating gaze, and then said, with an affected carelessness of tone -

"Your preacher and your dreams have made you quite a moralist."

"They have not taken from my heart any of the love it has felt for you," said Margaret, tears coming into her eyes.

"I know that, Margaret. You were always too kind and indulgent, and I always too wayward and unreasonable. But I am getting years on my side, and shall not always be a foolish girl."

Snow had now begun to fall thickly, and the late December day was waning toward the early twilight. Margaret went down stairs and left Irene alone in her chamber, where she remained until nearly tea-time before joining her father.

Mr. Delancy did not altogether feel satisfied in his mind about this unheralded visit from his daughter, with whose wayward moods he was too familiar. It might be all as she said, but there were intrusive misgivings that troubled him.

At tea-time she took her old place at the table in such an easy, natural way, and looked so pleased and happy, that her father was satisfied. He asked about her husband, and she talked of him without reserve.

"What day is Hartley coming up?" he inquired.

"I hope to see him on the day before Christmas," returned Irene. There was a falling in her voice that, to the ears of Mr. Delancy, betrayed a feeling of doubt.

"He will not, surely, put it off later," said the father.

"I don't know," said Irene. "He may be prevented from leaving early enough to reach here before Christmas morning. If there should be a cold snap, and the river freeze up, it will make the journey difficult and attended with delay."

"I think the winter has set in;" and Mr. Delancy turned his ear toward the window, against which the snow and hail were beating with violence. "It's a pity Hartley didn't come up with you."

A sober hue came over the face of Irene. This did not escape the notice of her father; but it was natural that she should feel sober in thinking of her husband as likely to be kept from her by the storm. That such were her thoughts her words made evident, for she said, glancing toward the window -

"If there should be a deep snow, and the boats stop running, how can Hartley reach here in time?"

On the next morning the sun rose bright and warm for the season. Several inches of snow had fallen, giving to the landscape a wintry whiteness, but the wind was coming in from the south, genial as spring. Before night half the snowy covering was gone.

"We had our fears for nothing," said Mr. Delancy, on the second day, which was as mild as the preceding one. "All things promise well. I saw the boats go down as usual; so the river is open still."

Irene did not reply. Mr. Delancy looked at her curiously, but her face was partly turned away and he did not get its true expression.

The twenty-fourth came. No letter had been received by Irene, nor had she written to New York since her arrival at Ivy Cliff.

"Isn't it singular that you don't get a letter from Hartley?" said Mr. Delancy.

Irene had been sitting silent for some time when her father made this remark.

"He is very busy," she said, in reply.

"That's no excuse. A man is never too busy to write to his absent wife."

"I haven't expected a letter, and so am not disappointed. But he's on his way, no doubt. How soon will the boat arrive?"

"Between two and three o'clock."

"And it's now ten."

The hours passed on, and the time of arrival came. The windows of Irene's chamber looked toward the river, and she was standing at one of them alone when the boat came in sight. Her face was almost colorless, and contracted by an expression of deep anxiety. She remained on her feet for the half hour that intervened before the boat could reach the landing. It was not the first time that she had watched there, in the excitement of doubt and fear, for the same form her eyes were now straining themselves to see.

The shrill sound of escaping steam ceased to quiver on the air, and in a few minutes the boat shot forward into view and went gliding up the river. Irene scarcely breathed, as she stood, with colorless face, parted lips and eager eyes, looking down the road that led to the landing. But she looked in vain; the form of her husband did not appear - and it was Christmas Eve!

What did it mean?

CHAPTER VII.

THE LETTER.

YES, what did it mean? Christmas Eve, and Hartley still absent?

Twilight was falling when Irene came down from her room and joined her father in the library. Mr. Delancy looked into her face narrowly as she entered. The dim light of the closing day was not strong enough to give him its true expression; but he was not deceived as to its troubled aspect.

"And so Hartley will not be here to-day," he said, in a tone that expressed both disappointment and concern.

"No. I looked for him confidently. It is strange."

There was a constraint, a forced calmness in Irene's voice that did not escape her father's notice.

"I hope he is not sick," said Mr. Delancy.

"Oh no." Irene spoke with a sudden earnestness; then, with failing tones, added -

"He should have been here to-day."

She sat down near the open grate, shading her face with a hand-screen, and remained silent and abstracted for some time.

"There is scarcely a possibility of his arrival to-night," said Mr. Delancy. He could not get his thoughts away from the fact of his son-in-law's absence.

"He will not be here to-night," replied Irene, a cold dead level in her voice, that Mr. Delancy well understood to be only a blind thrown up to conceal her deeply-disturbed feelings.

"Do you expect him to-morrow, my daughter?" asked Mr. Delancy, a few moments afterward, speaking as if from a sudden thought or a sudden purpose. There was a meaning in his tones that showed his mind to be in a state not prepared to brook evasion.

"I do," was the unhesitating answer; and she turned and looked calmly at her father, whose eyes rested with a fixed, inquiring gaze upon her countenance. But half her face was lit by a reflection from the glowing grate, while half lay in shadow. His reading, therefore was not clear.

If Irene had shown surprise at the question, her father would have felt better satisfied. He meant it as a probe; but if a tender spot was reached, she had the self-control not to give a sign of pain. At the tea-table Irene rallied her spirits and talked lightly to her father; it was only by an effort that he could respond with even apparent cheerfulness.

Complaining of a headache, Irene retired, soon after tea, to her room, and did not come down again during the evening.

The next day was Christmas. It rose clear and mild as a day in October. When Irene came down to breakfast, her pale, almost haggard, face showed too plainly that she had passed a night of sleeplessness and suffering. She said, "A merry Christmas," to her father, on meeting him, but there was no heart in the words. It was almost impossible to disguise the pain that almost stifled respiration. Neither of them did more than make a feint at eating. As Mr. Delancy arose from the table, he said to Irene -

"I would like to see you in the library, my daughter."

She followed him passively, closing the door behind her as she entered.

"Sit down. There." And Mr. Delancy placed a chair for her, a little way from the grate.

Irene dropped into the chair like one who moved by another's volition.

"Now, daughter," said Mr. Delancy, taking a chair, and drawing it in front of the one in which she was seated, "I am going to ask a plain question, and I want a direct answer."

Irene rallied herself on the instant.

"Did you leave New York with the knowledge and consent of your husband?"

The blood mounted to her face and stained it a deep crimson:

"I left without his knowledge. Consent I never ask."

The old proud spirit was in her tones.

"I feared as much," replied Mr. Delancy, his voice falling. "Then you do not expect Hartley to-day?"

"I expected him yesterday. He may be here to-day. I am almost sure he will come."

"Does he know you are here?"

"Yes."

"Why did you leave without his knowledge?"

"To punish him."

"Irene!"

"I have answered without evasion. It was to punish him."

"I do not remember in the marriage vows you took upon yourselves anything relating to punishments," said Mr. Delancy. "There were explicit things said of love and duty, but I do not recall a sentence that referred to the right of one party to punish the other."

Mr. Delancy paused for a few moments, but there was no reply to this rather novel and unexpected view of the case.

"Did you by anything in the rite acquire authority to punish your husband when his conduct didn't just suit your fancy?"

Mr. Delancy pressed the question.

"It is idle, father," said Irene, with some sharpness of tone, "to make an issue like this. It does not touch the case. Away back of marriage contracts lie individual rights, which are never surrendered. The right of self-protection is one of these; and if retaliation is needed as a guarantee of future peace, then the right to punish is included in the right of self-protection."

"A peace gained through coercion of any kind is not worth having. It is but the semblance of peace - is war in bonds," replied Mr. Delancy. "The moment two married partners begin the work of coercion and punishment, that moment love begins to fail. If love gives not to their hearts a common beat, no other power is strong enough to do the work. Irene, I did hope that the painful experiences already passed through would have made you wiser. It seems not, however. It seems that self-will, passion and a spirit of retaliation are to govern your actions, instead of patience and love. Well, my child, if you go on sowing this seed in your garden now, in the spring-time of life, you must not murmur when autumn gives you a harvest of thorns and thistles. If you sow tares in your field, you must not expect to find corn there when you put in your sickle to reap. You can take back your morning salutation. It is not a 'merry Christmas' to you or to me; and I think we are both done with merry Christmases."

"Father!"

The tone in which this word was uttered was almost a cry of pain.

"It is even so, my child - even so," replied Mr. Delancy, in a voice of irrepressible sadness. "You have left your husband a second time. It is not every man who would forgive the first offence; not one in twenty who would pardon the second. You are in great peril, Irene. This storm that you have conjured up may drive you to hopeless shipwreck. You need not expect Hartley to-day. He will not come. I have studied his character well, and know that he will not pass this conduct over lightly."

Even while this was said a servant, who had been over to the village, brought in a letter and handed it to Mr. Delancy, who, recognizing in the superscription the handwriting of his daughter's husband, broke the seal hurriedly. The letter was in these words:

"MY DEAR SIR: As your daughter has left me, no doubt with the purpose of finally abandoning the effort to live in that harmony so essential to happiness in married life, I shall be glad if you will choose some judicious friend to represent her in consultation with a friend whom I will select, with a view to the arrangement of a separation, as favorable to her in its provisions as it can possibly be made. In view of the peculiarity of our temperaments, we made a great error in this experiment. My hope was that love would be counselor to us both; that the law of mutual forbearance would have rule. But we are both too impulsive, too self-willed, too undisciplined. I do not pretend to throw all the blame on Irene. We are as flint and steel. But she has taken the responsibility of separation, and I am left without alternative. May God lighten the burden of pain her heart will have to bear in the ordeal through which she has elected to pass.

Your unhappy son,

"HARTLEY EMERSON."

Mr. Delancy's hand shook so violently before he had finished reading that the paper rattled in the air. On finishing the last sentence he passed it, without a word, to his daughter. It was some moments before the strong agitation produced by the sight of this letter, and its effect upon her father, could be subdued enough to enable her to read a line.

"What does it mean, father? I don't understand it," she said, in a hoarse, deep whisper, and with pale, quivering lips.

"It means," said Mr. Delancy, "that your husband has taken you at your word."

"At my word! What word?"

"You have left the home he provided for you, I believe?"

"Father!"

Her eyes stood out staringly.

"Let me read the letter for you." And he took it from her hand. After reading it aloud and slowly, he said -

"That is plain talk, Irene. I do not think any one can misunderstand it. You have, in his view, left him finally, and he now asks me to name a judicious friend to meet his friend, and arrange a basis of separation as favorable to you in its provisions as it can possibly be made."

"A separation, father! Oh no, he cannot mean that!" And she pressed her hands strongly against her temples.

"Yes, my daughter, that is the simple meaning."

"Oh no, no, no! He never meant that."

"You left him?"

"But not in that way; not in earnest. It was only in fitful anger - half sport, half serious."

"Then, in Heaven's name, sit down and write him so, and that without the delay of an instant. He has put another meaning on your conduct. He believes that you have abandoned him."

"Abandoned him! Madness!" And Irene, who had risen from her chair, commenced moving about the room in a wild, irresolute kind of way, something like an actress under tragic excitement.

"This is meant to punish me!" she said, stopping suddenly, and speaking in a voice slightly touched with indignation. "I understand it all, and see it as a great outrage. Hartley knows as well I do that I left as much in sport as in earnest. But this is carrying the joke too far. To write such a letter to you! Why didn't he write to me? Why didn't he ask me to appoint a friend to represent me in the arrangement proposed?"

"He understood himself and the case entirely," replied Mr. Delancy. " Believing that you had abandoned him -"

"He didn't believe any such thing!" exclaimed Irene, in strong excitement.

"You are deceiving yourself, my daughter. His letter is calm and deliberate. It was not written, as you can see by the date, until yesterday. He has taken time to let passion cool. Three days were permitted to elapse, that you might be heard from in case any change of purpose occurred. But you remained silent. You abandoned him."

"Oh, father, why will you talk in this way? I tell you that Hartley is only doing this to punish me; that he has no more thought of an actual separation than he has of dying."

"Admit this to be so, which I only do in the argument," said Mr. Delancy, "and what better aspect does it present?"

"The better aspect of sport as compared with earnest," replied Irene.

"At which both will continue to play until earnest is reached - and a worse earnest than the present. Take the case as you will, and it is one of the saddest and least hopeful that I have seen."

Irene did not reply.

"You must elect some course of action, and that with the least possible delay," said Mr. Delancy. "This letter requires an immediate answer. Go to your room and, in communion with God and your own heart, come to some quick decision upon the subject."

Irene turned away without speaking and left her father alone in the library.

CHAPTER VIII.

THE FLIGHT AND THE RETURN.

WE will not speak of the cause that led to this serious rupture between Mr. and Mrs. Emerson. It was light as vanity - an airy nothing in itself - a spark that would have gone out on a baby's cheek without leaving a sign of its existence. On the day that Irene left the home of her husband he had parted from her silent, moody and with ill-concealed anger. Hard words, reproaches and accusations had passed between them on the night previous; and both felt unusually disturbed. The cause of all this, as we have said, was light as vanity. During the day Mr. Emerson, who was always first to come to his senses, saw the folly of what had occurred, and when he turned his face homeward, after three o'clock, it was with the purpose of ending the unhappy state by recalling a word to which he had given thoughtless utterance.

The moment our young husband came to this sensible conclusion his heart beat with a freer motion and his spirits rose again into a region of tranquillity. He felt the old tenderness toward his wife returning, dwelt on her beauty, accomplishments, virtues and high mental endowments with a glow of pride, and called her defects of character light in comparison.

T. S. Arthur

"If I were more a man, and less a child of feeling and impulse," he said to himself, "I would be more worthy to hold the place of husband to a woman like Irene. She has strong peculiarities - who has not peculiarities? Am I free from them? She is no ordinary woman, and must not be trammeled by ordinary tame routine. She has quick impulses; therefore, if I love her, should I not guard them, lest they leap from her feebly restraining hand in the wrong direction? She is sensitive to control; why, then, let her see the hand that must lead her, sometimes, aside from the way she would walk through the promptings of her own will? Do I not know that she loves me? And is she not dear to me as my own life? What folly to strive with each other! What madness to let angry feelings shadow for an instant our lives!"

It was in this state of mind that Emerson returned home. There were a few misgivings in his heart as he entered, for he was not sure as to the kind of reception Irene would offer his overtures for peace; but there was no failing of his purpose to sue for peace and obtain it. With a quick step he passed through the hall, and, after glancing into the parlors to see if his wife were there, went up stairs with two or three light bounds. A hurried glance through the chambers showed him that they had no occupant. He was turning to leave them, when a letter, placed upright on a bureau, attracted his attention. He caught it up. It was addressed to him in the well-known hand of his wife. He opened it and read:

"I leave for Ivy Cliff to-day. IRENE."

Two or three times Emerson read the line - "I leave for Ivy Cliff to-day" - and looked at the signature, before its meaning came fully into his thought.

"Gone to Ivy Cliff!" he said, at last, in a low, hoarse voice. "Gone, and without a word of intimation or explanation! Gone, and in the heat of anger! Has it come to this, and so soon! God help us!" And the unhappy man sunk into a chair, heart-stricken and weak as a child.

For nearly the whole of the night that followed he walked the floor of his room, and the next day found him in a feverish condition of both mind and body. Not once did the thought of following his wife to Ivy Cliff, if it came into his mind, rest there for a moment. She had gone home to her father with only an announcement of the fact. He would wait some intimation of her further purpose; but, if they met again, she must come back to him. This was his first, spontaneous conclusion; and it was not questioned in his thought, nor did he waver from it an instant. She must come back of her own free will, if she came back at all.

It was on the twentieth day of December that Irene left New York. Not until the twenty-second could a letter from her reach Hartley, if, on reflection or after conference with her father, she desired to make a communication. But the twenty-second came and departed without a word from the absent one. So did the twenty-third. By this time Hartley had grown very calm, self-adjusted and resolute. He had gone over and over again the history of their lives since marriage bound them together, and in this history he could see nothing hopeful as bearing on the future. He was never certain of Irene. Things said and done in moments of thoughtlessness or excitement, and not meant to hurt or offend, were constantly disturbing their peace. It was clouds, and rain, and fitful sunshine all the while. There were no long seasons of serene delight.

"Why," he said to himself, "seek to prolong this effort to blend into one two lives that seem hopelessly antagonistic. Better stand as far apart as the antipodes than live in perpetual strife. If I should go to Irene, and, through concession or entreaty, win her back again, what guarantee would I have for the future? None, none whatever. Sooner or later we must be driven asunder by the violence of our ungovernable passions, never to draw again together. We are apart now, and it is well. I shall not take the first step toward a reconciliation."

Hartley Emerson was a young man of cool purpose and strong will. For all that, he was quick-tempered and undisciplined. It was from the possession of these qualities that he was steadily advancing in his profession, and securing a practice at the bar which promised to give him a high position in the future. Persistence was another element of his character. If he adopted any course of conduct, it was a difficult thing to turn him aside. When he laid his hand upon the plough, he was of those who rarely look back. Unfortunate qualities these for a crisis in life such as now existed.

On the morning of the twenty-fourth of December, no word having come from his wife, Emerson coolly penned the letter to Mr. Delancy which is given in the preceding chapter, and mailed it so that it would reach him on Christmas day. He was in earnest - sternly in earnest - as Mr. Delancy, on reading his letter, felt him to be. The honeymoon flight was one thing; this abandonment of a husband's home, another thing.

Emerson gave to them a different weight and quality. Of the first act he could never think without a burning cheek - a sense of mortification - a pang of wounded pride; and long ere this he had made up his mind that if Irene ever left him again, it would be for ever, so far as perpetuity depended on his action in the case. He would never follow her nor seek to win her back.

Yes, he was in earnest. He had made his mind up for the worst, and was acting with a desperate coolness only faintly imagined by Irene on receipt of his letter to her father. Mr. Delancy, who understood Emerson's character better, was not deceived. He took the communication in its literal meaning, and felt appalled at the ruin which impended.

Emerson passed the whole of Christmas day alone in his house. At meal-times he went to the table and forced himself to partake lightly of food, in order to blind the servants, whose curiosity in regard to the absence of Mrs. Emerson was, of course, all on the alert. After taking tea he went out.

His purpose was to call upon a friend in whom he had great confidence, and confide to him the unhappy state of his affairs. For an hour he walked the streets in debate on the propriety of this course. Unable, however, to see the matter clearly, he returned home with the secret of his domestic trouble still locked in his own bosom.

It was past eight o'clock when he entered his dwelling. A light was burning in one of the parlors, and he stepped into the room. After walking for two or three times the length of the apartment, Mr. Emerson threw himself on a sofa, a deep sigh escaping his lips as he

T. S. Arthur

did so. At the same moment he heard a step in the passage, and the rustling of a woman's garments, which caused him to start again to his feet. In moving his eyes met the form of Irene, who advanced toward him, and throwing her arms around his neck, sobbed,

"Dear husband! can you, will you forgive my childish folly?"

His first impulse was to push her away, and he, even grasped her arms and attempted to draw them from his neck. She perceived this, and clung to him more eagerly.

"Dear Hartley!" she said, "will you not speak to me ?"

"Irene!" His voice was cold and deep, and as he pronounced her name he withdrew himself from her embrace. At this she grew calm and stepped a pace back from him.

"Irene, we are not children," he said, in the same cold, deep voice, the tones of which were even and measured. "That time is past. Nor foolish young lovers, who fall out and make up again twice or thrice in a fortnight; but man and wife, with the world and its sober realities before us."

"Oh, Hartley," exclaimed Irene, as he paused; "don't talk to me in this way! Don't look at me so! It will kill me. I have done wrong. I have acted like foolish child. But I am penitent. It was half in sport that I went away, and I was so sure of seeing you at Ivy Cliff yesterday that I told father you were coming."

" Irene, sit down." And Emerson took the hand of his

wife and led her to a sofa. Then, after closing the parlor door, he drew a chair and seated himself directly in front of her. There was a coldness and self-possession about him, that chilled Irene.

"It is a serious thing," he said, looking steadily in her face, "for a wife to leave, in anger, her husband's house for that of her father."

She tried to make some reply and moved her lips in attempted utterance, but the organs of speech refused to perform their office.

"You left me once before in anger, and I went after you. But it was clearly understood with myself then that if you repeated the act it would be final in all that appertained to me; that unless you returned, it would be a lifelong separation. You *have* repeated the act; and, knowing your pride and tenacity of will, I did not anticipate your return. And so I was looking the sad, stern future in the face as steadily as possible, and preparing to meet it as a man conscious of right should be prepared to meet whatever trouble lies in store for him. I went out this evening, after passing the Christmas day alone, with the purpose of consulting an old and discreet friend as to the wisest course of action. But the thing was too painful to speak of yet. So I came back - and you are here!"

She looked at him steadily while he spoke, her face white as marble, and her colorless lips drawn back from her teeth.

"Irene," he continued, "it is folly for us to keep on in the way we have been going. I am wearied out, and you cannot be happy in a relation that is for ever reminding you that your own will and thought are no longer sole arbiters of action; that there is another will and another thought that must at times be consulted, and even obeyed. I am a man, and a husband; you a woman, and a wife, - we are equal as to rights and duties - equal in the eyes of God; but to the man and husband appertains a certain precedence in action; consent, co-operation and approval, if he be a thoughtful and judicious man, appertaining to the wife."

As Emerson spoke thus, he noticed a sign of returning warmth in her pale face, and a dim, distant flash in her eyes. Her proud spirit did not accept this view of their relation to each other. He went on:

"If a wife has no confidence in her husband's manly judgment, if she cannot even respect him, then the case is altered. She must be understanding and will to herself; must lead both him and herself if he be weak enough to consent. But the relation is not a true one; and marriage, under this condition of things, is only a semblance."

"And that is your doctrine?" said Irene. There was a shade of surprise in her voice that lingered huskily in her throat.

"That is my doctrine," was Emerson's firmly spoken answer.

Irene sighed heavily. Both were silent for some moments. At length Irene said, lifting her hands and bringing them down with an action of despair,

"In bonds! in bonds!"

"No, no!" Her husband replied quickly and earnestly. "Not in bonds, but in true freedom, if you will - the freedom of reciprocal action."

"Like bat and ball," she answered, with bitterness in her tones.

"No, like heart and lungs," he returned, calmly. "Irene! dear wife! Why misunderstand me? I have no wish to rule, and you know I have never sought to place you in bonds. I have had only one desire, and that is to be your husband in the highest and truest sense. But, I am a man - you a woman. There are two wills and two understandings that must act in the same direction. Now, in the nature of things, the mind of one must, helped by the mind of the other to see right, take, as a general thing, the initiative where action is concerned. Unless this be so, constant collisions will occur. And this takes us back to the question that lies at the basis of all order and happiness - which of the two minds shall lead?"

"A man and his wife are equal," said Irene, firmly. The strong individuality of her character was asserting its claims even in this hour of severe mental pain.

"Equal in the eyes of God, as I have said before, but where action is concerned one must take precedence of the other, for, it cannot be, seeing that their office and duties are different, that their judgment in the general affairs of life can be equally clear. A man's work takes him out into the world, and throws him into sharp collision with other men. He learns, as a consequence, to think carefully and with deliberation, and to decide with caution, knowing that action, based on erroneous conclusions, may ruin his prospects in an hour. Thus,

T. S. Arthur

like the oak, which, grows up exposed to all elemental changes, his judgment gains strength, while his perceptions, constantly trained, acquire clearness. But a woman's duties lie almost wholly within this region of strife and action, and she remains, for the most part, in a tranquil atmosphere. Allowing nothing for a radical difference in mental constitution, this difference of training must give a difference of mental power. The man's judgment in affairs generally must be superior to the woman's, and she must acquiesce in its decisions or there can be no right union in marriage."

"Must lose herself in him," said Irene, coldly. "Become a cypher, a slave. That will not suit me, Hartley!" And she looked at him with firmly compressed mouth and steady eyes.

It came to his lips to reply, "Then you had better return to your father," but he caught the words back ere they leaped forth into sound, and, rising, walked the floor for the space of more than five minutes, Irene not stirring from the sofa. Pausing at length, he said in a voice which had lost its steadiness:

"You had better go up to your room, Irene. We are not in a condition to help each other now."

Mrs. Emerson did not answer, but, rising, left the parlor and went as her husband had suggested. He stood still, listening, until the sound of her steps and the rustle of her garments had died away into silence, when he commenced slowly walking the parlor floor with his head bent down, and continued thus, as if he had forgotten time and place, for over an hour. Then, awakened to consciousness by a sense of dizziness and exhaustion, he laid himself upon a sofa, and, shutting his eyes, tried to arrest the current of his troubled thoughts and sink into sleep and forgetfulness.

T. S. Arthur

CHAPTER IX.

THE RECONCILIATION.

FOR such a reception the young wife was wholly unprepared. Suddenly her husband had put on a new character and assumed a right of control against which her sensitive pride and native love of freedom arose in strong rebellion. That she had done wrong in going away she acknowledged to herself, and had acknowledged to him. But he had met confession in a spirit so different from what was anticipated, and showed an aspect so cold, stern, and exacting, that she was bewildered. She did not, however, mistake the meaning of his language. It was plain that she understood the man's position to be one of dictation and control: we use the stronger aspect in which it was presented to her mind. As to submission, it was not in all her thoughts. Wrung to agony as her heart was, and appalled as she looked, trembling and shrinking into the future, she did not yield a moment to weakness.

Midnight found Irene alone in her chamber. She had flung herself upon a bed when she came up from the parlor, and fallen asleep after an hour of fruitless beating about in her mind. Awaking from a maze of troubled dreams, she started up and gazed, half fearfully, around the dimly-lighted room.

"Where am I?" she asked herself. Some moments elapsed before the painful events of the past few days began to reveal themselves to her consciousness.

"And where is Hartley?" This question followed as soon as all grew clear. Sleep had tranquilized her state, and restored a measure of just perception. Stepping from the bed, she went from the room and passed silently down stairs. A light still burned in the parlor where she had left her husband some hours before, and streamed out through the partly opened door. She stood for some moments, listening, but there was no sound of life within. A sudden fear crept into her heart. Her hand shook as she laid it upon the door and pressed it open. Stepping within, she glanced around with a frightened air.

On the sofa lay Hartley, with his face toward the light. It was wan and troubled, and the brows were contracted as if from intense pain. For some moments Irene stood looking at him; but his eyes were shut and he lay perfectly still. She drew nearer and bent down over him. He was sleeping, but his breath came so faintly, and there was so little motion of his chest, that the thought flashed through her with an electric thrill that he might be dying! Only by a strong effort of self-control did she repress a cry of fear, or keep back her hands from clasping his neck. In what a strong tide did love rush back upon her soul! Her heart overflowed with tenderness, was oppressed with yearning.

"Oh, Hartley, my husband, my dear husband!" she cried out, love, fear, grief and anguish blending wildly in her voice, as she caught him in her arms and awoke him with a rain of tears and kisses.

"Irene! Love! Darling! What ails you? Where are we?" were the confusedly uttered sentences of Mr. Emerson, as he started from the sofa and, holding his young wife from him, looked into her weeping face.

"Call me again 'love' and 'darling,' and I care not where we are!" she answered, in tones of passionate entreaty. "Oh, Hartley, my dear, dear husband! A desert island, with you, would be a paradise; a paradise, without you, a weary desert! Say the words again. Call me 'darling!'" And she let her head fall upon his bosom.

"God bless you!" he said, laying his hand upon her head. He was awake and clearly conscious of place and position. His voice was distinct, but tremulous and solemn. "God bless you, Irene, my wife!"

"And make me worthy of your love," she responded faintly.

"Mutually worthy of each other," said he. "Wiser - better - more patient and forbearing. Oh, Irene," and his voice grew deep and tender, "why may we not be to each other all that our hearts desire?"

"We can - we must - we will!" she answered, lifting her hidden face from his bosom and turning it up fondly to his. "God helping me, I will be to you a better wife in the future."

"And I a more patient, loving, and forbearing husband," he replied. "Oh that our hearts might beat together as one heart!"

For a little while Irene continued to gaze into her husband's countenance with looks of the tenderest love, and then hid her face on his bosom again.

And thus were they again reconciled.

T. S. Arthur

CHAPTER X.

AFTER THE STORM.

AFTER the storm. And they were reconciled. The clouds rolled back; the sun came out again with his radiant smiles and genial warmth. But was nothing broken? nothing lost? Did each flower in the garden of love lift its head as bravely as before? In every storm of passion something is lost. Anger is a blind fury, who tramples ruthlessly on tenderest and holiest things. Alas for the ruin that waits upon her footsteps!

The day that followed this night of reconciliation had many hours of sober introversion of thought for both Emerson and his wife; hours in which memory reproduced language, conduct and sentiments that could not be dwelt upon without painful misgivings for the future. They understood each other too well to make light account of things said and done, even in anger.

In going over, as Irene did many times, the language used by her husband on the night before, touching their relation as man and wife, and his prerogative, she felt the old spirit of revolt arising. She tried to let her thought fall into his rational presentation of the question involving precedence, and even said to herself that he was right; but pride was strong, and kept lifting itself in her mind. She saw, most clearly, the hardest aspect of the case. It was, in her view, command and obedience. And she knew that submission was, for her, impossible.

On the part of Emerson, the day's sober thought left his mind in no more hopeful condition than that of his wife. The pain suffered in consequence of her temporary flight from home, though lessened by her return, had not subsided. A portion of confidence in her was lost. He felt that he had no guarantee for the future; that at any moment, in the heat of passion, she might leave him again. He remembered, too distinctly, her words on the night before, when he tried to make her comprehend his view of the relation between man and wife - "That will not suit me, Hartley." And he felt that she was in earnest; that she would resist every effort he might make to lead and control as a man in certain things, just as she had done from the beginning.

In matrimonial quarrels you cannot kiss and make up again, as children do, forgetting all the stormy past in the sunshiny present. And this was painfully clear to both Hartley and Irene, as she, alone in her chamber, and he, alone in his office, pondered, on that day of reconciliation, the past and the future. Yet each resolved to be more forbearing and less exacting; to be emulous of concession, rather than exaction; to let love, uniting with reason, hold pride and self-will in close submission.

Their meeting, on Hartley's return home, at his usual late hour in the afternoon, was tender, but not full of the joyous warmth of feeling that often showed itself. Their hearts were not light enough for ecstasy. But they were marked in their attentions to each other,

　　　　　　　　T. S. Arthur

emulous of affectionate words and actions, yielding and considerate. And yet this mutual, almost formal, recognition of a recent state of painful antagonism left on each mind a feeling of embarrassment, checked words and sentences ere they came to utterance, and threw amid their pleasant talks many intermittent pauses.

Often through the day had Mr. Emerson, as he dwelt on the unhappy relation existing between himself and his wife, made up his mind to renew the subject of their true position to each other, as briefly touched upon in their meeting of the night before, and as often changed his purpose, in fear of another rupture. Yet to him it seemed of the first importance that this matter, as a basis of future peace, should be settled between them, and settled at once. If he held one view and she another, and both were sensitive, quick-tempered and tenacious of individual freedom, fierce antagonism might occur at any moment. He had come home inclined to the affirmative side of the question, and many times during the evening it was on his lips to introduce the subject. But he was so sure that it would prove a theme of sharp discussion, that he had not the courage to risk the consequences.

There was peace again after this conflict, but it was not, by any means, a hopeful peace. It had no well-considered basis. The causes which had produced a struggle were still in existence, and liable to become active, by provocation, at any moment. No change had taken place in the characters, dispositions, temperaments or general views of life in either of the parties. Strife had ceased between them only in consequence of the pain it involved. A deep conviction of this fact so sobered the mind of Mr. Emerson, and altered, in consequence, his manner toward Irene, that she felt its reserve and coldness as a rebuke that chilled the warmth of her tender impulses.

And this manner did not greatly change as the days and weeks moved onward. Memory kept too vividly in the mind of Emerson that one act, and the danger of its repetition on some sudden provocation. He could not feel safe and at ease with his temple of peace built close to a slumbering volcano, which was liable at any moment to blaze forth and bury its fair proportions in lava and ashes.

Irene did not comprehend her husband's state of mind. She felt painfully the change in his manner, but failed in reaching the true cause. Sometimes she attributed his coldness to resentment; sometimes to defect of love; and sometimes to a settled determination on his part to inflict punishment. Sometimes she spent hours alone, weeping over these sad ruins of her peace, and sometimes, in a spirit of revolt, she laid down for herself a line of conduct intended to react against her husband. But something in his calm, kind, self-reliant manner, when she looked into his face, broke down her purpose. She was afraid of throwing herself against a rock which, while standing immovable, might bruise her tender limbs or extinguish life in the strong concussion.

CHAPTER XI.

A NEW ACQUAINTANCE.

BOTH Emerson and his wife came up from this experience changed in themselves and toward each other. A few days had matured them beyond what might have been looked for in as many years. Life suddenly put on more sober hues, and the future laid off its smiles and beckonings onward to greener fields and mountain-heights of felicity. There was a certain air of manly self-confidence, a firmer, more deliberate way of expressing himself on all subjects, and an evidence of mental clearness and strength, which gave to Irene the impression of power and superiority not wholly agreeable to her self-love, yet awakening emotions of pride in her husband when she contrasted him with other men. As a man among men, he was, as he had ever been, her beau ideal; but as a husband, she felt a daily increasing spirit of resistance and antagonism, and it required constant watchfulness over herself to prevent this feeling from exhibiting itself in act.

On the part of Emerson, the more he thought about this subject of the husband's relative duties and prerogatives - thought as a man and as a lawyer - the more strongly did he feel about it, and the more tenacious of his assumed rights did he become. Matters which seemed in the beginning of such light importance as scarcely to attract his attention, now loomed up before him as things of moment. Thus, if he spoke of their doing some particular thing in a certain way, and Irene suggested a different way, instead of yielding to her view, he would insist upon his own. If she tried to show him a reason why her way was best, he would give no weight to her argument or representation. On the other hand, it is but just to say that he rarely opposed her independent suggestions or interfered with her freedom; and if she had been as considerate toward him, the danger of trouble would have been lessened.

It is the little foxes that spoil the tender grapes, and so it is the little reactions of two spirits against each other that spoil the tender blossoms of love and destroy the promised vintage. Steadily, day by day, and week by week, were these light reactions marring the happiness of our undisciplined young friends, and destroying in them germ after germ, and bud after bud, which, if left to growth and development, would have brought forth ripe, luscious fruit in the later summer of their lives. Trifles, light as air were noticed, and their importance magnified. Words, looks, actions, insignificant in themselves, were made to represent states of will or antagonism which really had no existence.

Unhappily for their peace, Irene had a brooding disposition. She held in her memory utterances and actions forgotten by her husband, and, by dwelling upon, magnified and gave them an importance to which they were not entitled. Still more unhappily for their peace, Irene met about this time, and became attached to, a lady of fine intellectual attainments and fascinating manners, who was an extremist in opinion

T. S. Arthur

on the subject of sexual equality. She was married, but to a man greatly her inferior, though possessing some literary talent, which he managed to turn to better account than she did her finer powers. He had been attracted by her brilliant qualities, and in approaching her scorched his wings, and ever after lay at her feet. She had no very high respect for him, but found a husband on many accounts a convenient thing, and so held on to the appendage. If he had been man enough to remain silent on the themes she was so fond of discussing on all occasions, people of common sense and common perception would have respected him for what he was worth. But he gloried in his bondage, and rattled his chains as gleefully as if he were discoursing sweet music. What she announced oracularly, he attempted to demonstrate by bald and feeble arguments. He was the false understanding to her perverted will.

The name of this lady was Mrs. Talbot. Irene met her soon after her marriage and removal to New York, and was charmed with her from the beginning. Mr. Emerson, on the contrary, liked neither her nor her sentiments, and considered her a dangerous friend for his wife. He expressed himself freely in regard to her at the commencement of the intimacy; but Irene took her part so warmly, and used such strong language in her favor, that Emerson deemed it wisest not to create new sentiments in her favor out of opposition to himself.

Within a week from that memorable Christmas day on which Irene came back from Ivy Cliff, Mrs. Talbot, who had taken a fancy to the spirited, independent, undisciplined wife of Emerson, called in to see her new friend. Irene received her cordially. She was, in fact, of all her acquaintances, the one she most desired to meet.

"I'm right glad you thought of making me a call," said Mrs. Emerson, as they sat down together. "I've felt as dull all the morning as an anchorite."

"You dull!" Mrs. Talbot affected surprise, as she glanced round the tasteful room in which they were sitting. "What is there to cloud your mind? With such a home and such a husband as you possess life ought to be one long, bright holiday."

"Good things in their way," replied Mrs. Emerson. "But not everything."

She said this in a kind of thoughtless deference to Mrs. Talbot's known views on the subject of homes and husbands, which she had not hesitated to call women's prisons and women's jailers.

"Indeed! And have you made that discovery?"

Mrs. Talbot laughed a low, gurgling sort of laugh, leaning, at the same time, in a confidential kind of way, closer to Mrs. Emerson.

"Discovery!"

"Yes."

"It is no discovery," said Mrs. Emerson. "The fact is self-evident. There is much that a woman needs for happiness beside a home and a husband."

"Right, my young friend, right!" Mrs. Talbot's manner

grew earnest. "No truer words were ever spoken. Yes - yes - a woman needs a great deal more than these to fill the measure of her happiness; and it is through the attempt to restrict and limit her to such poor substitutes for a world-wide range and freedom that she has been so dwarfed in mental stature, and made the unhappy creature and slave of man's hard ambition and indomitable love of power. There were Amazons of old - as the early Greeks knew to their cost - strong, self-reliant, courageous women, who acknowledged no human superiority. Is the Amazonian spirit dead in the earth? Not so! It is alive, and clothing itself with will, power and persistence. Already it is grasping the rein, and the mettled steed stands impatient to feel the rider's impulse in the saddle. The cycle of woman's degradation and humiliation is completed. A new era in the world's social history has dawned for her, and the mountain-tops are golden with the coming day."

Irene listened with delight and even enthusiasm to these sentiments, uttered with ardor and eloquence.

"It is not woman's fault, taking her in the aggregate, that she is so weak in body and mind, and such a passive slave to man's will," continued Mrs. Talbot. "In the retrocession of races toward barbarism mere muscle, in which alone man is superior to woman, prevailed. Physical strength set itself up as master. Might made right. And so unhappy woman was degraded below man, and held to the earth, until nearly all independent life has been crushed out of her. As civilization has lifted nation after nation out of the dark depths of barbarism, the condition of woman physically has been improved. For the sake of his children, if from no better motive, man has come to treat his wife with a more considerate kindness. If she is still but the hewer of his wood and the drawer of his water, he has, in many cases, elevated her to the position of dictatress in these humble affairs. He allows her 'help!' But, mentally and socially, he continues to degrade her. In law she is scarcely recognized, except as a criminal. She is punished if she does wrong, but has no legal protection in her rights as an independent human being. She is only man's shadow. The public opinion that affects her is made by him. The earliest literature of a country is man's expression; and in this man's view of woman is always apparent. The sentiment is repeated generation after generation, and age after age, until the barbarous idea comes down, scarcely questioned, to the days of high civilization, culture and refinement.

"Here, my young friend, you have the simple story of woman's degradation in this age of the world. Now, so long as she submits, man will hold her in fetters. Power and dominion are sweet. If a man cannot govern a state, he will be content to govern a household - but govern he will, if he can find anywhere submissive subjects."

"He is born a tyrant; that I have always felt," said Mrs. Emerson. "You see it in a family of sisters and brothers. The boys always attempt to rule their sisters, and if the latter do not submit, then comes discord and contention."

"I have seen this, in hundreds of instances," replied Mrs. Talbot. "It was fully illustrated in my own case. I had two brothers, who undertook to exercise their love of domineering on me. But they did not find a passive subject - no, not by any means. I was never obedient to their will, for I had one of my own. We made the house often a bedlam for our poor mother; but I never gave way - no, not for an instant, come what might. I had different stuff in me from that of common girls, and in time the boys were glad to let me alone."

"Are your brothers living?" asked Mrs. Emerson.

"Yes. One resides in New York, and the other in Boston. One is a merchant, the other a physician."

"How was it as you grew older?"

"About the same. They are like nearly all men - despisers of woman's intellect."

Irene sighed, and, letting her eyes fall to the floor, sat lost in thought for some moments. The suggestions of her friend were not producing agreeable states of mind.

"They reject the doctrine of an equality in the sexes?" said Mrs. Emerson.

"Of course. All men do that," replied Mrs. Talbot.

"Your husband among the rest?"

"Talbot? Oh, he's well enough in his way!" The lady spoke lightly, tossing her head in a manner that involved both indifference and contempt. "I never take him into account when discussing these matters. That point was settled between us long and long ago. We jog on without trouble. Talbot thinks as I do about the women - or pretends that he does, which is all the same."

"A rare exception to the general run of husbands," said

Irene, thinking at the same time how immeasurably superior Mr. Emerson was to this weakling, and despising him in her heart for submitting to be ruled by a woman. Thus nature and true perception spoke in her, even while she was seeking to blind herself by false reasonings.

"Yes, he's a rare exception; and it's well for us both that it is so. If he were like your husband, for instance, one of us would have been before the legislature for a divorce within twelve months of our marriage night."

"Like my husband! What do you mean?" Mrs. Emerson drew herself up, with half real and half affected surprise.

"Oh, he's one of your men who have positive qualities about them - strong in intellect and will."

Irene felt pleased with the compliment bestowed upon her husband.

"But wrong in his ideas of woman."

"How do you know?" asked Irene.

"How do I know? As I know all men with whom I come in contact. I probe them."

"And you have probed my husband?"

"Undoubtedly."

"And do not regard him as sound on this subject?"

"No sounder than other men of his class. He regards

woman as man's inferior."

"I think you state the case too strongly," said Mrs. Emerson, a red spot burning on her cheek. "He thinks them mentally different."

"Of course he does."

"But not different as to superiority and inferiority," replied Irene.

"Mere hair-splitting, my child. If they are mentally different, one must be more highly organized than the other, and of course, superior. Mr. Emerson thinks a man's rational powers stronger than a woman's, and that, therefore, he must direct in affairs generally, and she follow his lead. I know; I've talked with and drawn him out on this subject."

Mrs. Emerson sighed again faintly, while her eyes dropped from the face of her visitor and sunk to the floor. A shadow was falling on her spirit - a weight coming down with a gradually increasing pressure upon her heart. She remembered the night of her return from Ivy Cliff and the language then used by her husband on this very subject, which was mainly in agreement with the range of opinions attributed to him by Mrs. Talbot.

"Marriage, to a spirited woman," she remarked, in a pensive undertone, "is a doubtful experiment."

"Always," returned her friend. "As woman stands now in the estimate of man, her chances for happiness are almost wholly on the side of old-maidism. Still, freedom is the price of struggle and combat; and woman will first have to show, in actual strife, that she is the equal of her present lord."

"Then you would turn every home into a battlefield?" said Mrs. Emerson.

"Every home in which there is a tyrant and an oppressor," was the prompt answer. "Many fair lands, in all ages, have been trampled down ruthlessly by the iron feet of war; and that were better, as the price of freedom, than slavery."

Irene sighed again, and was again silent.

"What," she asked, "if the oppressor is so much stronger than the oppressed that successful resistance is impossible? that with every struggle the links of the chain that binds her sink deeper into her quivering flesh?"

"Every age and every land have seen noble martyrs in the cause of freedom. It is better to die for liberty than live an ignoble slave," answered the tempter.

"And I will die a free woman." This Irene said in her heart.

CHAPTER XII.

IN BONDS.

SENTIMENTS like these, coming to Irene as they did while she was yet chafing under a recent collision with her husband, and while the question of submission was yet an open one, were near proving a quick-match to a slumbering mine in her spirit, and had not her husband been in a more passive state than usual, there might have been an explosion which would have driven them asunder with such terrific force that reunion must have been next to impossible.

It would have been well if their effects had died with the passing away of that immediate danger. But as we think so we incline to act. Our sentiments are our governors; and of all imperious tyrants, false sentiments are the most ruthless. The beautiful, the true, the good they trample out of the heart with a fiery malignity that knows no touch of pity; for the false is the bitter enemy of the true and makes with it no terms of amity.

The coldness which had followed their reconciliation might have gradually given way before the warmth of genuine love, if Irene had been left to the counsels of her own heart; if there had been no enemy to her peace, like Mrs. Talbot, to throw in wild, vague thoughts of oppression and freedom among the half-developed opinions which were forming in her mind. As it was, a jealous scrutiny of words and actions took the place of that tender confidence which was coming back to Irene's heart, and she became watchfully on the alert; not, as she might have been, lovingly ministrant.

Only a few days were permitted to elapse after the call of this unsafe friend before Irene returned the visit, and spent two hours with her, conning over the subject of woman's rights and woman's wrongs. Mrs. Talbot introduced her to writers on the vexed question, who had touched the theme with argument, sarcasm, invective and bold, brilliant, specious generalities; read to her from their books; commented on their deductions, and uttered sentiments on the subject of reform and resistance as radical as the most extreme.

"We must agitate - we must act - we must do good deeds of valor and self-sacrifice for our sex," she said, in her enthusiastic way. "Every woman, whether of high or low condition, of humble powers or vigorous intellect, has a duty to perform, and she is false to the honor and rights of her sex if she do not array herself on the side of freedom. You have great responsibilities resting upon you, my young friend. I say it soberly, even solemnly. Responsibilities which may not be disregarded without evil consequences to yourself and others. You are young, clear-thoughted and resolute - have will, purpose and endurance. You are married to a young man destined, I think, to make his mark in the world; but, as I have said before, a false education has given him erroneous ideas on this great and important subject. Now what is your duty?"

The lady paused as if for an answer.

"What is your duty, my dear young friend?" she repeated.

"I will answer for you," she continued. "Your duty is to be true to yourself and to your sisters in bonds."

"In bonds! *I* in bonds!" Mrs. Talbot touched her to the quick.

"Are you a free woman?" The inquiry was calmly made.

Irene started to the floor and moved across the room, then turned and came back again. Her cheeks burned and her eyes flashed. She stood before Mrs. Talbot and looked at her steadily.

"The question has disturbed you?" said the lady.

"It has," was the brief answer.

"Why should it disturb you?"

Irene did not answer.

"I can tell you."

"Say on."

"You are in bonds, and feel the fetters."

"Mrs. Talbot!"

"It is so, my poor child, and you know it as well as I do. From the beginning of our acquaintance I have seen this ; and more than once, in our various conversations, you have admitted the fact."

"I?"

"Yes, you."

Irene let her thoughts run back through the sentiments and opinions which she had permitted herself to utter in the presence of her friend, to see if she had so fully betrayed herself. She could not recall the distinct language, but it was plain that Mrs. Talbot had her secret, and therefore reserve on the subject was useless.

"Well," she said, after standing for some time before Mrs. Talbot, "if I am in bonds, it is not because I do not worship freedom."

"I know that," was the quickly-spoken answer. "And it is because I wish to see you a free woman that I point to your bonds. Now is the time to break them - now, before years have increased their strength - now, before habit has made tyranny a part of your husband's nature. He is your ruler, because the social sentiment is in favor of manly domination. There is hope for you now, and now only. You must begin the work of reaction while both are young. Let your husband understand, from this time, that you are his equal. It may go a little hard at first. He will, without doubt, hold on to the reins, for power is sweet; but if there be true love for you in his heart, he will yield in the struggle, and make you his companion and equal, as you should be. If his love be not genuine, why -"

She checked herself. It might be going a step too far with her young friend to utter the thought that was coming to her lips. Irene did not question her as to what more she was about to say. There was stimulus enough in the words already spoken. She felt all the strength of her nature rising into opposition.

"Yes, I will be free," she said in her heart. "I will be his equal, not his slave."

"It may cost you some pain in the beginning," resumed the tempter.

"I am not afraid of pain," said Irene.

"A brave heart spoke there. I wish we had more on our side with the stuff you are made of. There would be hope of a speedier reform than is now promised."

"Heaven send the reform right early! It cannot come a day too soon." Irene spoke with rising ardor.

"It will be our own fault," said Mrs. Talbot, "if we longer bow our necks to the yoke or move obedient to our task-masters. Let us lay the axe to the very root of this evil and hew it down."

"Even if we are crushed by the tree in falling," responded Irene, in the spirit of a martyr.

From this interview our wrong-directed young friend went home with more clearly defined purposes touching her conduct toward her husband than she had hitherto entertained. She saw him in a new aspect, and in a character more definitely outlined. He loomed up in more colossal proportions, and put on sterner features. All disguises were thrown away, and he stood forth, not a loving husband, but the tyrant of her home.

Weak, jealous, passion-tost child! how this strong, self-willed, false woman of the world had bewildered her thoughts, and pushed her forth into an arena of strife, where she could only beat about blindly, and hurt herself and others, yet accomplish no good.

From her interview with Mrs. Talbot, Irene went home, bearing more distinct ideas of resistance in her mind. In this great crisis of her life she felt that she needed just such a friend, who could give direction to her striving spirit, and clothe for her in thoughts the native impulses that she knew only as a love of freedom. She believed now that she understood herself better than before, and comprehended more clearly her duties and responsibilities.

It was in this mood of mind that she met her husband when he returned in the afternoon from his office. Happily for them, he was in a quiet, non-resistant state, and in a special good-humor with himself and the world. Professional matters had shaped themselves to his wishes, and left his mind at peace. Irene had, in consequence, everything pretty much her own way. Hartley did not fail to notice a certain sharpness of manner about her, and a certain spiciness of sentiment when the subject of their intermittent talks verged on themes relating to women; but he felt no inclination whatever for argument or opposition, and so her arrows struck a polished shield, and went gracefully and harmlessly aside.

"Shall we go and have a merry laugh with Matthews to-night?" said Hartley, as they sat at the tea-table. "I feel just in the humor."

"No, I thank you," replied Irene, curtly. "I don't incline

T. S. Arthur

to the laughing mood, just now."

"Laughing is contagious," suggested Hartley.

"I shall not take the infection to-night." And she balanced her little head with the perpendicularity of a plumb-line.

"Can't I persuade you?" He was in a real good-humor, and smiled as he said this.

"No, sir. You may waive both argument and persuasion. I am in earnest."

"And when a woman is in earnest you might as well essay to move the Pillars of Hercules."

"You might as well in my case," answered Irene, without any softening of tone or features.

"Then I shall not attempt, after a hard day's work, a task so difficult. I am in a mood for rest and quiet," said the young husband.

"Perhaps," he resumed, after a little pause, "you may feel somewhat musical. There is to be a vocal and instrumental concert to-night. What say you to going there? I think I could enjoy some good singing, mightily."

Irene closed her lips firmly, and shook her head.

"Not musically inclined this evening?"

"No," she replied.

"Got a regular stay-at-home feeling?"

"Yes."

"Enough," said Hartley, with unshadowed good-humor, "we will stay at home."

And he sung a snatch of the familiar song - "There's no place like home," rising, as he did so, from the table, and offering Irene his arm. She could do no less than accept the courtesy, and so they went up to their cozy sitting-room arm-in-arm - he chatty, and she almost silent.

"What's the matter, petty?" he asked, in a fond way, after trying for some time, but in vain, to draw her out into pleasant conversation. "Ain't you well to-night?"

Now, so far as her bodily state was concerned, Irene never felt better in her life. So she could not plead indisposition.

"I feel well," she replied, glancing up into her husband's face in a cold, embarrassed kind of way.

"Then your looks belie your condition - that's all. If it isn't the body, it must be the mind. What's gone wrong, darling?"

The tenderness in Hartley's tones was genuine, and the heart of Irene leaped to his voice with a responsive throe. But was he not her master and tyrant? How that thought chilled the sweet impulse!

"Nothing wrong," she answered, with a sadness of tone which she was unable to conceal. "But I feel dull, and cannot help it."

"You should have gone with me to laugh with Matthews. He would have shaken all these cobwebs from your brain. Come! it is not yet too late."

But the rebel spirit was in her heart; and to have acceded to he husband's wishes would have been to submit herself to control.

"You must excuse me," she replied. "I feel as if home were the better place for me to-night."

An impatient answer was on her tongue; but she checked its utterance, and spoke from a better spirit.

Not even as a lover had Hartley shown more considerate tenderness than marked all his conduct toward Irene this evening. His mind was in a clear-seeing region, and his feelings tranquil. The sphere of her antagonism failed to reach him. He did not understand the meaning of her opposition to his wishes, and so pride, self-love and self-will remained quiescent. How peacefully unconscious was he of the fact that his feet were standing over a mine, and that a single spark of passion struck from him would have sprung that mine in fierce explosion! He read to Irene from a volume which he knew to be a favorite; talked to her about Ivy Cliff and her father; suggested an early visit to the pleasant old river home; and thus charmed away the evil spirits which had found a lodgment in her bosom.

But how different it might have been!

CHAPTER XIII.

THE REFORMERS.

SOCIAL theories that favor our passions, peculiarities, defects of character or weaknesses are readily adopted, and, with minds of an ardent temper, often become hobbies. There is a class of persons who are never content with riding their own hobbies; they must have others mount with them. All the world is going wrong because it moves past them - trotting, pacing or galloping, as it may be, upon its own hobbies. And so they try to arrest this movement or that, or, gathering a company of aimless people, they galvanize them with their own wild purposes, and start them forth into the world on Quixotic errands.

These persons are never content to wait for the slow changes that are included in all orderly developments. Because a thing seems right to them in the abstract, it must be done now. They cannot wait for old things to pass away, as preliminary to the inauguration of what is new.

"If I had the power," we have heard one of this class say, "evil and sorrow and pain should cease from the earth in a moment." And in saying this the thought was not concealed that God had this power, but failed to exercise it. With them no questions of expediency, no regard for time-endowed prejudices, no weak spirit of waiting, no looking for the fullness of time could have any influence. What they willed to be done must be done now; and they were impatient and angry at every one who stood in their way or opposed their theories.

In most cases, you will find these "reformers," as they generally style themselves, governed more by a love of ruling and influencing others than by a spirit of humanity. They are one-sided people, and can only see one side of a subject in clear light. It matters little to them what is destroyed, so that they can build. If they possess the gift of language, either as writers or talkers - have wit, brilliancy and sarcasm - they make disciples of the less gifted, and influence larger or smaller circles of men and women. Flattered by this homage to their talents, they grow more ardent in the cause which they have espoused, and see, or affect to see, little else of any importance in the world. They do some good and much harm. Good, in drawing general attention to social evils that need reforming - evil, in causing weak people to forget common duties in their ambition to set the world right.

There is always danger in breaking suddenly away from the regular progression of things and taking the lead in some new and antagonistic movement. Such things must and will be; but they who set up for social reformers must be men and women of pure hearts, clear minds and the broadest human sympathies. They must be lovers of their kind, not lovers of themselves; brave as patriots, not as soldiers of fortune who seek for booty and renown.

Not many of these true reformers - all honor to them! - are found among the noisy coteries that infest the land

and turn so many foolish people away from real duties.

One of the dangers attendant on association with the class to which we refer lies in the fact that they draw around them certain free-thinking, sensual personages, of no very stable morality, who are ready for anything that gives excitement to their morbid conditions of mind. Social disasters, of the saddest kind, are constantly occurring through this cause. Men and women become at first unsettled in their opinions, then unsettled in their conduct, and finally throw off all virtuous restraint.

Mrs. Talbot, the new friend of Mrs. Emerson, belonged to the better sort of reformers in one respect. She was a pure-minded woman; but this did not keep her out of the circle of those who were of freer thought and action. Being an extremist on the subject of woman's social position, she met and assimilated with others on the basis of a common sentiment. This threw her in contact with many from whom she would have shrunk with instinctive aversion had she known their true quality. Still, the evil to her was a gradual wearing away, by the power of steady attrition, of old, true, conservative ideas in regard to the binding force of marriage. There was always a great deal said on this subject, in a light way, by persons for whose opinions on other subjects she had the highest respect, and this had its influence. Insensibly her views and feelings changed, until she found herself, in some cases, the advocate of sentiments that once would have been rejected with instinctive repugnance.

This was the woman who was about acquiring a strong influence over the undisciplined, self-willed and too self-reliant young wife of Hartley Emerson; and this

T. S. Arthur

was the class of personages among whom her dangerous friend was about introducing her. At the house of Mrs. Talbot, where Irene became a frequent visitor, she met a great many brilliant, talented and fascinating people, of whom she often spoke to her husband, for she was too independent to have any concealments. She knew that he did no like Mrs. Talbot, but this rather inclined her to a favorable estimation, and really led to a more frequent inter-course than would otherwise have been the case.

Once a week Mrs. Talbot held a kind of conversazione, at which brilliant people and people with hobbies met to hear themselves talk. Mr. and Mrs. Emerson had a standing invitation to be present at these reunions, and, as Irene wished to go, her husband saw it best not to interpose obstacles. Besides, as he knew that she went to Mrs. Talbot's often in the day-time, and met a good many people there, he wished to see for himself who they were, and judge for himself as to their quality. Of the men who frequented the parlors of Mrs. Talbot, the larger number had some prefix to their names, as Professor, Doctor, Major, or Colonel. Most of the ladies were of a decidedly literary turn - some had written books, some were magazine contributors, one was a physician, and one a public lecturer. Nothing against them in all this, but much to their honor if their talents and acquirements were used for the common good.

The themes of conversation at these weekly gatherings were varied, but social relations and social reform were in most cases the leading topics. Two or three evenings at Mrs. Talbot's were enough to satisfy Mr. Emerson that the people who met there were not of a character to exercise a good influence upon his wife. But how was he to keep her from associations that evidently presented strong attractions? Direct opposition he feared to make, for the experience of a few months had been sufficient to show him that she would resist all attempts on his part to exercise a controlling influence.

He tried at first to keep her away by feigning slight indisposition, or weariness, or disinclination to go out, and so lead her to exercise some self-denial for his sake. But her mind was too firmly bent on going to be turned so easily from its purpose; she did not consider trifles like these of sufficient importance to interfere with the pleasures of an evening at one of Mrs. Talbot's conversaziones. Mr. Emerson felt hurt at his wife's plain disregard of his comfort and wishes, and said within himself, with bitterness of feeling, that she was heartless.

One day, at dinner-time, he said to her -

"I shall not be able to go to Mrs. Talbot's to-night."

"Why?" Irene looked at her husband in surprise, and with a shade of disappointment on her countenance.

"I have business of importance with a gentleman who resides in Brooklyn, and have promised to meet him at his house this evening."

"You might call for me on your return," said Irene.

"The time of my return will be uncertain. I cannot now tell how late I may be detained in Brooklyn."

"I'm sorry." And Irene bent down her eyes in a thoughtful way. "I promised Mrs. Talbot to be there to-night," she added.

"Mrs. Talbot will excuse you when she knows why you were absent."

"I don't know about that," said Irene.

"She must be a very unreasonable woman," remarked Emerson.

"That doesn't follow. You could take me there, and Mrs. Talbot find me an escort home."

"Who?" Emerson knit his brows and glanced sharply at his wife. The suggestion struck him unpleasantly.

"Major Willard, for instance;" and she smiled in a half-amused, half-mischievous way.

"You cannot be in earnest, surely?" said Emerson.

"Why not?" queried his wife, looking at her husband with calm, searching eyes.

"You would not, in the first place, be present there, unaccompanied by your husband; and, in the second place, I hardly think my wife would be seen in the street, at night, on the arm of Major Willard."

Mr. Emerson spoke like a man who was in earnest.

"Do you know anything wrong of Major Willard?" asked Irene.

"I know nothing about him, right or wrong," was replied. "But, if I have any skill in reading men, he is very far from being a fine specimen."

"Why, Hartley! You have let some prejudice come in to warp your estimation."

"No. I have mixed some with men, and, though my opportunity for observation has not been large, I have met two or three of your Major Willards. They are polished and attractive on the surface, but unprincipled and corrupt."

"I cannot believe this of Major Willard," said Irene.

"It might be safer for you to believe it," replied Hartley.

"Safer! I don't understand you! You talk in riddles? How safer?"

Irene showed some irritation.

"Safer as to your good name," replied her husband.

"My good name is in my own keeping" said the young wife, proudly.

"Then, for Heaven's sake, remain its safe custodian," replied Emerson. "Don't let even the shadow of a man like Major Willard fall upon it."

"I am sorry to see you so prejudiced," said Irene, coldly; "and sorry, still further, that you have so poor an opinion of your wife."

"You misapprehend me," returned Hartley. "I am neither prejudiced nor suspicious. But seeing danger in your way, as a prudent man I lift a voice of warning. I am out in the world more than you are, and see more of its worst side. My profession naturally opens to me doors of observation that are shut to many. I see the inside of character, where others look only upon the fair outside."

"And so learn to be suspicious of everybody," said Irene.

"No; only to read indices that to many others are unintelligible."

"I must learn to read them also."

"It would be well if your sex and place in the world gave the right opportunity," replied Hartley.

"Truly said. And that touches the main question. Women, immured as they now are, and never suffered to go out into the world unless guarded by husband, brother or discreet managing friend, will continue as weak and undiscriminating as the great mass of them now are. But, so far as I am concerned, this system is destined to change. I must be permitted a larger liberty, and opportunities for independent observation. I wish to read character for myself, and make up my own mind in regard to the people I meet."

"I am only sorry," rejoined her husband, "that your first effort at reading character and making up independent opinions in regard to men and principles had not found scope in another direction. I am afraid that, in trying to get close enough to the people you meet at Mrs. Talbot's for accurate observation, you will draw so near to dangerous fires as to scorch your garments."

"Complimentary to Mrs. Talbot!"

"The remark simply gives you my estimate of some of her favored visitors."

"And complimentary to your wife," added Irene.

"My wife," said Hartley, in a serious voice, "is, like myself, young and inexperienced, and should be particularly cautious in regard to all new acquaintances - men or women - particularly if they be some years her senior, and particularly if they show any marked desire to cultivate her acquaintance. People with a large worldly experience, like most of those we have met at Mrs. Talbot's, take you and I at disadvantage. They read us through at a single sitting, while it may take us months, even years, to penetrate the disguises they know so well how to assume."

"Nearly all of which, touching the pleasant people we meet at Mrs. Talbot's, is assumed," replied Irene, not at all moved by her husband's earnestness.

"You may learn to your sorrow, when the knowledge comes too late," he responded, "that even more than I have assumed is true."

"I am not in fear of the sorrow," was answered lightly.

As Irene, against all argument, persuasion and remonstrance on the part of her husband, persisted in her determination to go to Mrs. Talbot's, he engaged a carriage to take her there and to call for her at eleven o'clock.

" Come away alone , " he said , with impressive

earnestness, as he parted from her. "Don't let any courteous offer induce you to accept an attendant when you return home."

CHAPTER XIV.

A STARTLING EXPERIENCE.

MRS. EMERSON did not feel altogether comfortable in mind as she rode away from her door alone. She was going unattended by her husband, and against his warmly-spoken remonstrance, to pass an evening with people of whom she knew but little, and against whom he had strong prejudices.

"It were better to have remained at home," she said to herself more than once before her arrival at Mrs. Talbot's. The marked attentions she received, as well from Mrs. Talbot as from several of her guests, soon brought her spirits up to the old elevation. Among those who seemed most attracted by her was Major Willard, to whom reference has already been made.

"Where is your husband?" was almost his first inquiry on meeting her. "I do not see him in the room."

"He had to meet a gentleman on business over in Brooklyn this evening," replied Irene.

"Ah, business!" said the major, with a shrug, a movement of the eyebrows and a motion in the corners of his mouth which were not intelligible signs to Mrs. Emerson. That they meant something more than he

T. S. Arthur

was prepared to utter in words, she was satisfied, but whether of favorable or unfavorable import touching her absent husband, she could not tell. The impression on her mind was not agreeable, and she could not help remembering what Hartley had said about the major.

"I notice," remarked the latter, "that we have several ladies here who come usually without their husbands. Gentlemen are not always attracted by the feast of reason and the flow of soul. They require something more substantial. Oysters and terrapin are nearer to their fancy."

"Not more to my husband's fancy," replied Mrs. Emerson, in a tone of vindication, as well as rebuke at such freedom of speech.

"Beg your pardon a thousand times, madam!" returned Major Willard, "if I have even seemed to speak lightly of one who holds the honored position of your husband. Nothing could have been farther from my thought. I was only trifling."

Mrs. Emerson smiled her forgiveness, and the major became more polite and attentive than before. But his attentions were not wholly agreeable. Something in the expression of his eyes as he looked at her produced an unpleasant repulsion. She was constantly remembering some of the cautions spoken by Hartley in reference to this man, and she wished scores of times that he would turn his attentions to some one else. But the major seemed to have no eyes for any other lady in the room.

In spite of the innate repulsion to which we have referred, Mrs. Emerson was flattered by the polished major's devotion of himself almost wholly to her during the evening, and she could do no less in return than make herself as agreeable as possible.

At eleven o'clock she had notice that her carriage was at the door. The major was by, and heard the communication. So, when she came down from the dressing-room, he was waiting for her in the hall, ready cloaked and gloved.

"No, Major Willard, I thank you," she said, on his making a movement to accompany her. She spoke very positively.

"I cannot see you go home unattended." And the major bowed with graceful politeness.

"Oh no," said Mrs. Talbot. "You must not leave my house alone. Major, I shall expect you to attend my young friend."

It was in vain that Mrs. Emerson objected and remonstrated, the gallant major would listen to nothing; and so, perforce, she had to yield. After handing her into the carriage, he spoke a word or two in an undertone to the driver, and then entering, took his place by her side.

Mrs. Emerson felt strangely uncomfortable and embarrassed, and shrunk as far from her companion as the narrow space they occupied would permit; while he, it seemed to her, approached as she receded. There was a different tone in his voice when he spoke as the carriage moved away from any she had noticed heretofore. He drew his face near to hers in speaking, but the rattling of the wheels made hearing difficult. He had, during the evening, referred to a star actress then occupying public attention, of whom some scandalous things had been said, and declared his belief in her innocence. To Mrs. Emerson's surprise - almost disgust - his first remark after they were seated in the carriage was about this actress. Irene did not respond to his remark.

"Did you ever meet her in private circles?" he next inquired.

"No, sir," she answered, coldly.

"I have had that pleasure," said Major Willard.

There was no responsive word.

"She is a most fascinating woman," continued the major. "That Juno-like beauty which so distinguishes her on the stage scarcely shows itself in the drawing-room. On the stage she is queenly - in private, soft, voluptuous and winning as a houri. I don't wonder that she has crowds of admirers."

The major's face was close to that of his companion, who felt a wild sense of repugnance, so strong as to be almost suffocating. The carriage bounded as the wheels struck an inequality in the street, throwing them together with a slight concussion. The major laid his hand upon that of Mrs. Emerson, as if to support her. But she instantly withdrew the hand he had presumed to touch. He attempted the same familiarity again, but she placed both hands beyond the possibility of accidental or designed contact with his, and shrank still closer into the corner of the carriage, while her heart fluttered and a tremor ran through her frame.

Major Willard spoke again of the actress, but Mrs. Emerson made no reply.

"Where are we going?" she asked, after the lapse of some ten minutes, glancing from the window and seeing, instead of the tall rows of stately houses which lined the streets along the whole distance between Mrs. Talbot's residence and her own house, mean-looking tenements.

"The driver knows his route, I presume," was answered.

"This is not the way, I am sure," said Mrs. Emerson, a slight quiver of alarm in her voice.

"Our drivers know the shortest cuts," replied the major, "and these do not always lead through the most attractive quarters of the town."

Mrs. Emerson shrunk back again in her seat and was silent. Her heart was throbbing with a vague fear. Suddenly the carriage stopped and the driver alighted.

"This is not my home," said Mrs. Emerson, as the driver opened the door, and the major stepped out upon the pavement.

"Oh, yes. This is No. 240 L - street. Yes, ma'am," added the driver, "this is the number that the gentleman told me."

"What gentleman?" asked Mrs. Emerson.

"This gentleman, if you please, ma'am."

"Drive me home instantly, or this may cost you dear!" said Mrs. Emerson, in as stern a voice as surprise and fear would permit her to assume.

"Madam - " Major Willard commenced speaking.

"Silence, sir! Shut the door, driver, and take me home instantly!"

The major made a movement as if he were about to enter the carriage, when Mrs. Emerson said, in a low, steady, threatening voice -

"At your peril, remain outside! Driver, shut the door. If you permit that man to enter, my husband will hold you to a strict account."

"Stand back!" exclaimed the driver, in a resolute voice.

But the major was not to be put off in this way. He did not move from the open door of the carriage. In the next moment the driver's vigorous arm had hurled him across the pavement. The door was shut, the box mounted and the carriage whirled away, before the astonished man could rise, half stunned, from the place where he fell. A few low, bitter, impotent curses fell from his lips, and then he walked slowly away, muttering threats of vengeance.

It was nearly twelve o'clock when Irene reached home.

"You are late," said her husband, as she came in.

"Yes," she replied, "later than I intended."

" What's the matter ? " he inquired , looking at

her narrowly.

"Why do you ask?" She tried to put on an air of indifference.

"You look pale and your voice is disturbed."

"The driver went through parts of the town in returning that made me feel nervous, as I thought of my lonely and unprotected situation."

"Why did he do that?"

"It wasn't to make the way shorter, for the directest route would have brought me home ten minutes ago. I declare! The fellow's conduct made me right nervous. I thought a dozen improbable things."

"It is the last time I will employ him," said Hartley. "How dare he go a single block away from a direct course, at this late hour?" He spoke with rising indignation.

At first, Irene resolved to inform her husband of Major Willard's conduct, but it will be seen by this conversation that she had changed her mind, at least for the present. Two or three things caused her to hesitate until she could turn the matter over in her thoughts more carefully. Pride had its influence. She did not care to admit that she had been in error and Hartley right as to Major Willard. But there was a more sober aspect of the case. Hartley was excitable, brave and strong-willed. She feared the consequences that might follow if he were informed of Major Willard's outrageous conduct. A personal collision she saw to be almost inevitable in this event. Mortifying publicity, if not the shedding of blood, would ensue.

So, for the present at least, she resolved to keep her own secret, and evaded the close queries of her husband, who was considerably disturbed by the alleged conduct of the driver.

One good result followed this rather startling experience. Irene said no more about attending the conversaziones of Mrs. Talbot. She did not care to meet Major Willard again, and as he was a regular visitor at Mrs. Talbot's, she couldn't go there without encountering him. Her absence on the next social evening was remarked by her new friend, who called on her the next day.

"I didn't see you last night," said the agreeable Mrs. Talbot.

"No, I remained at home," replied Mrs. Emerson, the smile with which she had received her friend fading partly away.

"Not indisposed, I hope?"

"No."

"But your husband was! Talk it right out, my pretty one!" said Mrs. Talbot, in a gay, bantering tone. "Indisposed in mind. He don't like the class of people one meets at my house. Men of his stamp never do."

It was on the lips of Mrs. Emerson to say that there might be ground for his dislike of some who were met there. But she repressed even a remote reference to an affair that, for the gravest of reasons, she still desired to keep as her own secret. So she merely answered -

"The indisposition of mind was on my part."

"On your part? Oh dear! That alters the case. And, pray, what occasioned this indisposition? Not a previous mental surfeit, I hope."

"Oh no. I never get a surfeit in good company. But people's states vary, as you are aware. I had a stay-at-home feeling last night, and indulged myself."

"Very prettily said, my dear. I understand you entirely, and like your frank, outspoken way. This is always best with friends. I desire all of mine to enjoy the largest liberty - to come and see me when they feel like it, and to stay away when they don't feel like coming. We had a delightful time. Major Willard was there. He's a charming man! Several times through the evening he asked for you. I really think your absence worried him. Now, don't blush! A handsome, accomplished man may admire a handsome and accomplished woman, without anything wrong being involved. Because one has a husband, is she not to be spoken to or admired by other men? Nonsense! That is the world's weak prudery, or rather the common social sentiment based on man's tyranny over woman."

As Mrs. Talbot ran on in this strain, Mrs. Emerson had time to reflect and school her exterior. Toward Major Willard her feelings were those of disgust and detestation. The utterance of his name shocked her womanly delicacy, but when it was coupled with a sentiment of admiration for her, and an intimation of the probable existence of something reciprocal on her part, it was with difficulty that she could restrain a burst of indignant feeling. But her strong will helped her, and she gave no intelligible sign of what was really passing in her thoughts. The subject being altogether disagreeable, she changed it as soon as possible.

In this interview with Mrs. Talbot a new impression in regard to her was made on the mind of Mrs. Emerson. Something impure seemed to pervade the mental atmosphere with which she was surrounded, and there seemed to be things involved in what she said that shadowed a latitude in morals wholly outside of Christian duty. When they separated, much of the enthusiasm which Irene had felt for this specious, unsafe acquaintance was gone, and her power over her was in the same measure lessened.

CHAPTER XV.

CAPTIVATED AGAIN.

BUT it is not so easily escaping from a woman like Mrs. Talbot, when an acquaintanceship is once formed. In less than a week she called again, and this time in company with another lady, a Mrs. Lloyd, whom she introduced as a very dear friend. Mrs. Lloyd was a tall, spare woman, with an intellectual face, bright, restless, penetrating eyes, a clear musical voice, subdued, but winning manners. She was a little past thirty, though sickness of body or mind had stolen the bloom of early womanhood, and carried her forward, apparently, to the verge of forty. Mrs. Emerson had never before heard of this lady. But half an hour's conversation completely captivated her. Mrs. Lloyd had traveled through Europe, and spoke in a familiar way of the celebrated personages whom she had met abroad, - talked of art, music and architecture, literature, artists and literary men - displayed such high culture and easy acquaintance with themes quite above the range usually met with among ordinary people, that Mrs. Emerson felt really flattered with the compliment of a visit.

"My good friend, Mrs. Talbot," said Mrs. Lloyd, during their conversation, "has spoken of you so warmly that I could do no less than make overtures for an acquaintance, which I trust may prove agreeable. I anticipated the pleasure of seeing you at her house last week, but was disappointed."

"The interview of to-day," remarked Mrs. Talbot, coming in adroitly, "will only make pleasanter your meeting on to-morrow night."

"At your house?" said Mrs. Lloyd.

"Yes." And Mrs. Talbot threw a winning smile upon Mrs. Emerson. "You will be there?"

"I think not," was replied.

"Oh, but you must come, my dear Mrs. Emerson! We cannot do without you."

"I have promised my husband to go out with him."

"Your husband!" The voice of Mrs. Talbot betrayed too plainly her contempt of husbands.

"Yes, my husband." Mrs. Emerson let her voice dwell with meaning on the word.

The other ladies looked at each other for a moment or two with meaning glances; then Mrs. Talbot remarked, in a quiet way, but with a little pleasantry in her voice, as if she were not right clear in regard to her young friend's state of feeling,

"Oh dear! these husbands are dreadfully in the way, sometimes! Haven't you found it so, Mrs. Lloyd?"

The eyes of Mrs. Emerson were turned instantly to the

face of her new acquaintance. She saw a slight change of expression in her pale face that took something from its agreeable aspect. And yet Mrs. Lloyd smiled as she answered, in a way meant to be pleasant,

"They are very good in their place."

"The trouble," remarked Mrs. Talbot, in reply, "is to make them keep their place."

"At our feet." Mrs. Emerson laughed as she said this.

"No," answered Mrs. Lloyd - "at our sides, as equals."

"And beyond that," said Mrs. Talbot, "we want them to give us as much freedom in the world as they take for themselves. They come in and go out when they please, and submit to no questioning on our part. Very well; I don't object; only I claim the same right for myself. 'I will ask my husband.' Don't you hear this said every day? Pah! I'm always tempted to cut the acquaintance of a woman when I hear these words from her lips. Does a man, when a friend asks him to do anything or go anywhere, say, 'I'll ask my wife?' Not he. A lady who comes occasionally to our weekly reunions, but whose husband is too much of a man to put himself down to the level of our set, is permitted the enjoyment of an evening with us, now and then, on one condition."

"Condition!" There was a throb of indignant feeling in the voice of Mrs. Lloyd.

"Yes, on condition that no male visitor at my house shall accompany her home. A carriage is sent for her precisely at ten o'clock, when she must leave, and alone."

"Humiliating!" ejaculated Mrs. Lloyd.

"Isn't it? I can scarcely have patience with her. Major Willard has, at my instance, several times made an effort to accompany her, and once actually entered her carriage. But the lady commanded him to retire, or she would leave the carriage herself. Of course, when she took that position, the gallant major had to leave the field."

"Such a restriction would scarce have suited my fancy," said Mrs. Lloyd.

"Nor mine. What do you think of that?" And Mrs. Talbot looked into the face of Mrs. Emerson, whose color had risen beyond its usual tone.

"Circumstances alter cases," replied the latter, crushing out all feeling from her voice and letting it fall into a dead level of indifference.

"But circumstances don't alter facts, my dear. There are the hard facts of restrictions and conditions, made by a man, and applied to his equal, a woman. Does she say to him, You can't go to your club unless you return alone in your carriage, and leave the club-house precisely at ten o'clock? Oh no. He would laugh in her face, or, perhaps, consult the family physician touching her sanity."

This mode of putting the question rather bewildered the mind of our young wife, and she dropped her eyes from those of Mrs. Talbot and sat looking upon the floor in silence.

"Can't you get your husband to release you from this engagement of which you have spoken?" asked Mrs. Lloyd. "I should like above all things to meet you to-morrow evening."

Mrs. Emerson smiled as she answered,

"Husbands have rights, young know, as well as wives. We must consult their pleasure sometimes, as well as our own."

"Certainly - certainly." Mrs. Lloyd spoke with visible impatience.

"I promised to go with my husband to-morrow night," said Mrs. Emerson; "and, much as I may desire to meet you at Mrs. Talbot's, I am not at liberty to go there."

"In bonds! Ah me! Poor wives!" sighed Mrs. Talbot, in affected pity. "Not at liberty! The admission which comes to us from all sides."

She laughed in her gurgling, hollow way as she said this.

"Not bound to my husband, but to my word of promise," replied Mrs. Emerson, as pleasantly as her disturbed feelings would permit her to speak. The ladies were pressing her a little too closely, and she both saw and felt this. They were stepping beyond the bounds of reason and delicacy.

Mrs. Lloyd saw the state of mind which had been produced, and at once changed the subject.

"May I flatter myself with the prospect of having this

call returned?" she said, handing Mrs. Emerson her card as she was about leaving.

"It will give me great pleasure to know you better, and you may look to seeing me right early," was the bland reply. And yet Mrs. Emerson was not really attracted by this woman, but, on the contrary, repelled. There was something in her keen, searching eyes, which seemed to be looking right into the thoughts, that gave her a feeling of doubt.

"Thank you. The favor will be all on my side," said Mrs. Lloyd, as she held the hand of Mrs. Emerson and gave it a warm pressure.

The visit of these ladies did not leave the mind of Irene in a very satisfactory state. Some things that were said she rejected, while other things lingered and occasioned suggestions which were not favorable to her husband. While she had no wish to be present at Mrs. Talbot's on account of Major Willard, she was annoyed by the thought that Hartley's fixing on the next evening for her to go out with him was to prevent her attendance at the weekly conversazione.

Irene did not mention to her husband the fact that she bad received a visit from Mrs. Talbot, in company with a pleasant stranger, Mrs. Lloyd. It would have been far better for her if she had done so. Many times it was on her lips to mention the call, but as often she kept silent, one or the other of two considerations having influence. Hartley did not like Mrs. Talbot, and therefore the mention of her name, and the fact of her calling, would not be pleasant theme. The other consideration had reference to a woman's independence.

"He doesn't tell me of every man he meets through the day, and why should I feel under obligation to speak of every lady who calls?" So she thought. "As to Mrs. Lloyd, he would have a hundred prying question's to ask, as if I we not competent to judge of the character of my own friends and acquaintances?"

Within a week the call of Mrs. Lloyd was reciprocated by Mrs. Emerson; not in consequence of feeling drawn toward that lady, but she had promised to return the friendly visit, and must keep her word. She found her domiciliated in a fashionable boarding-house, and was received in the common parlor, in which were two or three ladies and a gentleman, besides Mrs. Lloyd. The greeting she received was warm, almost affectionate. In spite of the prejudice that was creeping into her mind in consequence of an unfavorable first impression, Mrs. Emerson was flattered by her reception, and before the termination of her visit she was satisfied that she had not, in the beginning, formed a right estimate of this really fascinating woman.

"I hope to see you right soon," she said, as she bade Mrs. Lloyd good-morning. "It will not be my fault if we do not soon know each other better."

"Nor mine either," replied Mrs. Lloyd. "I think I shall find you just after my own heart."

The voice of Mrs. Lloyd was a little raised as she said this, and Mrs. Emerson noticed that a gentleman who was in the parlor when she entered, but to whom she had not been introduced, turned and looked at her with a steady, curious gaze, which struck her at the time as being on the verge of impertinence.

Only two or three days passed before Mrs. Lloyd returned this visit. Irene found her more interesting than ever. She had seen a great deal of society, and had met, according to her own story, with most of the distinguished men and women of the country, about whom she talked in a very agreeable manner. She described their personal appearance, habits, peculiarities and manners, and related pleasant anecdotes about them. On authors and books she was entirely at home.

But there was an undercurrent of feeling in all she said that a wiser and more experienced woman than Irene would have noted. It was not a feeling of admiration for moral, but for intellectual, beauty. She could dissect a character with wonderful skill, but always passed the quality of goodness as not taken into account. In her view this quality did not seem to be a positive element.

When Mrs. Lloyd went away, she left the mind of Irene stimulated, restless and fluttering with vague fancies. She felt envious of her new friend's accomplishments, and ambitious to move in as wide a sphere as she had compassed. The visit was returned at an early period, and, as before, Mrs. Emerson met Mrs. Lloyd in the public parlor of her boarding-house. The same gentleman whose manner had a little annoyed her was present, and she noticed several times, on glancing toward him, that his eyes were fixed upon her, and with an expression that she did not understand.

After this, the two ladies met every day or two, and sometimes walked Broadway together. The only information that Mrs. Emerson had in regard to her attractive friend she received from Mrs. Talbot.

According to her statement, she was a widow whose married life had not been a happy one. The husband, like most husbands, was an overbearing tyrant, and the wife, having a spirit of her own, resisted his authority. Trouble was the consequence, and Mrs. Talbot thought, though she was not certain, that a separation took place before Mr. Lloyd's death. She had a moderate income, which came from her husband's estate, on which she lived in a kind of idle independence. So she had plenty of time to read, visit and enjoy herself in the ways her fancy or inclination might prompt.

CHAPTER XVI.

WEARY OF CONSTRAINT.

TIME moved on, and Mrs. Emerson's intimate city friends were those to whom she had been introduced, directly or indirectly, through Mrs. Talbot. Of these, the one who had most influence over her was Mrs. Lloyd, and that influence was not of the right kind. Singularly enough, it so happened that Mr. Emerson never let this lady at his house, though she spent hours there every week; and, more singular still, Irene had never spoken about her to her husband. She had often been on the point of doing so, but an impression that Hartley would take up an unreasonable prejudice against her kept the name of this friend back from her lips.

Months now succeeded each other without the occurrence of events marked by special interest. Mr. Emerson grew more absorbed in his profession as cases multiplied on his hands, and Irene, interested in her circle of bright-minded, independent-thoughted women, found the days and weeks gliding on pleasantly enough. But habits of estimating things a little differently from the common sentiment, and views of life not by any means consonant with those prevailing among the larger numbers of her sex, were gradually taking root.

Young, inexperienced, self-willed and active in mind, Mrs. Emerson had most unfortunately been introduced among a class of persons whose influence upon her could not fail to be hurtful. Their conversation was mainly of art, literature, social progress and development; the drama, music, public sentiment on leading topics of the day; the advancement of liberal ideas, the necessity of a larger liberty and a wider sphere of action for woman, and the equality of the sexes. All well enough, all to be commended when viewed in their just relation to other themes and interests, but actually pernicious when separated from the homely and useful things of daily life, and made so to overshadow these as to warp them into comparative insignificance. Here lay the evil. It was this elevation of her ideas above the region of use and duty into the mere æsthetic and reformatory that was hurtful to one like Irene - that is, in fact, hurtful to any woman, for it is always hurtful to take away from the mind its interest in common life - the life, we mean, of daily useful work.

Work! We know the word has not a pleasant sound to many ears, that it seems to include degradation, and a kind of social slavery, and lies away down in a region to which your fine, cultivated, intellectual woman cannot descend without, in her view, soiling her garments. But for all this, it is alone in daily useful work of mind or hands, work in which service and benefits to others are involved, that a woman (or a man) gains any true perfection of character. And this work must be her own, must lie within the sphere of her own relations to others, and she must engage in it from a sense of duty that takes its promptings from her own consciousness of right. No other woman can judge of her relation to this work, and she who dares to

T. S. Arthur

interfere or turn her aside should be considered an enemy - not a friend.

No wonder, if this be true, that we have so many women of taste, cultivation, and often brilliant intellectual powers, blazing about like comets or shooting stars in our social firmament. They attract admiring attention, excite our wonder, give us themes for conversation and criticism; but as guides and indicators while we sail over the dangerous sea of life, what are they in comparison with some humble star of the sixth magnitude that ever keeps its true place in the heavens, shining on with its small but steady ray, a perpetual blessing? And so the patient, thoughtful, loving wife and mother, doing her daily work for human souls and bodies, though her intellectual powers be humble, and her taste but poorly cultivated, fills more honorably her sphere than any of her more brilliant sisters, who cast off what they consider the shackles by which custom and tyranny have bound them down to mere home duties and the drudgery of household care. If down into these they would bring their superior powers, their cultivated tastes, their larger knowledge, how quickly would some desert homes in our land put on refreshing greenness, and desolate gardens blossom like the rose! We should have, instead of vast imaginary Utopias in the future, model homes in the present, the light and beauty of which, shining abroad, would give higher types of social life for common emulation.

Ah, if the Genius of Social Reform would only take her stand centrally! If she would make the regeneration of homes the great achievement of our day, then would she indeed come with promise and blessing. But, alas! she is so far vagrant in her habits - a fortune-telling gipsy, not a true, loving, useful woman.

Unhappily for Mrs. Emerson, it was the weird-eyed, fortune-telling gipsy whose Delphic utterances had bewildered her mind.

The reconciliation which followed the Christmas-time troubles of Irene and her husband had given both more prudent self-control. They guarded themselves with a care that threw around the manner of each a certain reserve which was often felt by the other as coldness. To both this was, in a degree, painful. There was tender love in their hearts, but it was overshadowed by self-will and false ideas of independence on the one side, and by a brooding spirit of accusation and unaccustomed restraint on the other. Many times, each day of their lives, did words and sentiments, just about to be uttered by Hartley Emerson, die unspoken, lest in them something might appear which would stir the quick feelings of Irene into antagonism.

There was no guarantee of happiness in such a state of things. Mutual forbearance existed, not from self-discipline and tender love, but from fear of conse-quences. They were burnt children, and dreaded, as well they might, the fire.

With little change in their relations to each other, and few events worthy of notice, a year went by. Mr. Delancy came down to New York several times during this period, spending a few days at each visit, while Irene went frequently to Ivy Cliff, and stayed there, occasionally, as long as two or three weeks. Hartley always came up from the city while Irene was at her father's, but never stayed longer than a single day, business requiring him to be at his office or in court.

Mr. Delancy never saw them together without closely observing their manner, tone of speaking and language. Both, he could see, were maturing rapidly. Irene had changed most. There was a style of thinking, a familiarity with popular themes and a womanly confidence in her expression of opinions that at times surprised him. With her views on some subjects his own mind was far from being in agreement, and they often had warm arguments. Occasionally, when her husband was at Ivy Cliff a difference of sentiment would arise between them. Mr. Delancy noticed, when this was the case, that Irene always pressed her view with ardor, and that her husband, after a brief but pleasant combat, retired from the field. He also noticed that in most cases, after this giving up of the contest by Hartley, he was more than usually quiet and seemed to be pondering things not wholly agreeable.

Mr. Delancy was gratified to see that there was no jarring between them. But he failed not at the same time to notice something else that gave him uneasiness. The warmth of feeling, the tenderness, the lover-like ardor which displayed itself in the beginning, no longer existed. They did not even show that fondness for each other which is so beautiful a trait in young married partners. And yet he could trace no signs of alienation. The truth was, the action of their lives had been inharmonious. Deep down in their hearts there was no defect of love. But this love was compelled to hide itself away; and so, for the most part, it lay concealed from even their own consciousness.

During the second year of their married life there came a change of state in both Irene and her husband. They had each grown weary of constraint when together. It was irksome to be always on guard, lest some word, tone or act should be misunderstood. In consequence, old collisions were renewed, and Hartley often grew impatient and even contemptuous toward his wife, when she ventured to speak of social progress, woman's rights, or any of the kindred themes in which she still took a warm interest. Angry retort usually followed on these occasions, and periods of coldness ensued, the effect of which was to produce states of alienation.

If a babe had come to soften the heart of Irene, to turn thought and feeling in a new direction, to awaken a mother's love with all its holy tenderness, how different would all have been! - different with her, and different with him. There would then have been an object on which both could centre interest and affection, and thus draw lovingly together again, and feel, as in the beginning, heart beating to heart in sweet accordings. They would have learned their love-lessons over again, and understood their meanings better. Alas that the angels of infancy found no place in their dwelling!

With no central attraction at home, her thoughts stimulated by association with a class of intellectual, restless women, who were wandering on life's broad desert in search of green places and refreshing springs, each day's journey bearing them farther and farther away from landscapes of perpetual verdure, Irene grew more and more interested in subjects that lay for the most part entirely out of the range of her husband's sympathies; while he was becoming more deeply absorbed in a profession that required close application of thought, intellectual force and clearness, and cold, practical modes of looking at all questions that came up for consideration. The consequence was that they were, in all their common interests, modes of thinking and habits of regarding the affairs of life, steadily receding from each other. Their evenings were now less frequently spent together. If home had been a pleasant place to him, Mr. Emerson would have usually remained at home after the day's duties were over; or, if he went abroad, it would have been usually in company with his wife. But home was getting to be dull, if not positively disagreeable. If a conversation was started, it soon involved disagreement in sentiment, and then came argument, and perhaps ungentle words, followed by silence and a mutual writing down in the mind of bitter things. If there was no conversation, Irene buried herself in a book - some absorbing novel, usually of the heroic school.

Naturally, under this state of things, Mr. Emerson, who was social in disposition, sought companionship else-where, and with his own sex. Brought into contact with men of different tastes, feelings and habits of thinking, he gradually selected a few as intimate friends, and, in association with these, formed, as his wife was doing, a social point of interest outside of his home; thus widening still further the space between them.

The home duties involved in housekeeping, indifferen-tly as they had always been discharged by Irene, were now becoming more and more distasteful to her. This daily care about mere eating and drinking seemed unworthy of a woman who had noble aspirations, such as burned in her breast. That was work for women-drudges who had no higher ambition; "and Heaven knows," she would often say to herself, "there are enough and to spare of these."

"What's the use of keeping up an establishment like

this just for two people?" she would often remark to her husband; and he would usually reply,

"For the sake of having a home into which one may retire and shut out the world."

Irene would sometimes suggest the lighter expense of boarding.

"If it cost twice as much I would prefer to live in my own house," was the invariable answer.

"But see what a burden of care it lays on my shoulders."

Now Hartley could only with difficulty repress a word of impatient rebuke when this argument was used. He thought of his own daily devotion to business, prolonged often into the night, when an important case was on hand, and mentally charged his wife with a selfish love of ease. On the other hand, it seemed to Irene that her husband was selfish in wishing her to bear the burdens of housekeeping just for his pleasure or convenience, when they might live as comfortably in a hotel or boarding-house.

On this subject Hartley would not enter into a discussion. "It's no use talking, Irene," he would say, when she grew in earnest. "You cannot tempt me to give up my home. It includes many things that with me are essential to comfort. I detest boarding-houses; they are only places for sojourning, not living."

As agreement on this subject was out of the question, Irene did not usually urge considerations in favor of abandoning their pleasant home.

CHAPTER XVII.

GONE FOR EVER!

ONE evening - it was nearly three years from the date of their marriage - Hartley Emerson and his wife were sitting opposite to each other at the centre-table, in the evening. She had a book in her hand and he held a newspaper before his face, but his eyes were not on the printed columns. He had spoken only a few words since he came in, and his wife noticed that he had the manner of one whose mind is in doubt or perplexity.

Letting the newspaper fall upon the table at length, Hartley looked over at his wife and said, in a quiet tone,

"Irene, did you ever meet a lady by the name of Mrs. Lloyd?"

The color mounted to the face of Mrs. Emerson as she replied,

"Yes, I have met her often."

"Since when?"

"I have known her intimately for the past two years."

"What!"

Emerson started to his feet and looked for some moments steadily at his wife, his countenance expressing the profoundest astonishment.

"And never once mentioned to me her name! Has she ever called here?"

"Yes."

"Often?"

"As often as two or three times a week."

"Irene!"

Mrs. Emerson, bewildered at first by her husband's manner of interrogating her, now recovered her self-possession, and, rising, looked steadily at him across the table.

"I am wholly at a loss to understand you," she now said, calmly.

"Have you ever visited that person at her boarding-house?" demanded Hartley.

"I have, often."

"And walked Broadway with her?"

"Certainly."

"Good heavens! can it be possible!" exclaimed the excited man.

"Pray, sir," said Irene, "who is Mrs. Lloyd?"

"An infamous woman!" was answered passionately.

"That is false!" said Irene, her eyes flashing as she spoke. "I don't care who says so, I pronounce the words false!"

Hartley stood still and gazed at his wife for some moments without speaking; then he sat down at the table from which he had arisen and, shading his face with his hands, remained motionless for a long time. He seemed like a man utterly confounded.

"Did you ever hear of Jane Beaufort?" he asked at length, looking up at his wife.

"Oh yes; everybody has heard of her."

"Would you visit Jane Beaufort?"

"Yes, if I believed her innocent of what the world charges against her."

"You are aware, then, that Mrs. Lloyd and Jane Beaufort are the same person?"

"No, sir, I am not aware of any such thing."

"It is true."

"I do not believe it. Mrs. Lloyd I have known intimately for over two years, and can verify her character."

"I am sorry for you, then, for a viler character it would

be difficult to find outside the haunts of infamy," said Emerson.

Contempt and anger were suddenly blended in his manner.

"I cannot hear one to whom I am warmly attached thus assailed. You must not speak in that style of my friends, Hartley Emerson!"

"Your friends!" There was a look of intense scorn on his face. "Precious friends, if she represent them, truly! Major Willard is another, mayhap?"

The face of Irene turned deadly pale at the mention of this name.

"Ha!"

Emerson bent eagerly toward his wife.

"And is that true, also?"

"What? Speak out, sir!" Irene caught her breath, and grasped the rein of self-control which had dropped, a moment, from her hands.

"It is said that Major Willard bears you company, at times, in your rides home from evening calls upon your precious friends."

"And you believe the story?"

"I didn't believe it," said Hartley, but in a tone that showed doubt.

"But have changed your mind?"

"If you say it is not true - that Major Willard never entered your carriage - I will take your word in opposition to the whole world's adverse testimony."

But Irene could not answer. Major Willard, as the reader knows, had ridden with her at night, and alone. But once, and only once. A few times since then she had encountered, but never deigned to recognize, him. In her pure heart the man was held in utter detestation.

Now was the time for a full explanation; but pride was aroused - strong, stubborn pride. She knew herself to stand triple mailed in innocency - to be free from weakness or taint; and the thought that a mean, base suspicion had entered the mind of her husband aroused her indignation and put a seal upon her lips as to all explanatory utterances.

"Then I am to believe the worst?" said Hartley, seeing that his wife did not answer. "The worst, and of you!"

The tone in which this was said, as well as the words themselves, sent a strong throb to the heart of Irene. "The worst, and of you!" This from her husband! and involving far more in tone and manner than in uttered language. "Then I am to believe the worst!" She turned the sentences over in her mind. Pride, wounded self-love, a smothered sense of indignation, blind anger, began to gather their gloomy forces in her mind. "The worst, and of you!" How the echoes of these words came back in constant repetition! "The worst, and of you!"

" How often has Major Willard ridden with you at

night?" asked Hartley, in a cold, resolute way.

No answer.

"And did you always come directly home?"

Hartley Emerson was looking steadily into the face of his wife, from which he saw the color fall away until it became of an ashen hue.

"You do not care to answer. Well, silence is significative," said the husband, closing his lips firmly. There was a blending of anger, perplexity, pain, sorrow and scorn in his face, all of which Irene read distinctly as she fixed her eyes steadily upon him. He tried to gaze back until her eyes should sink beneath his steady look, but the effort was lost; for not a single instant did they waver.

He was about turning away, when she arrested the movement by saying,

"Go on, Hartley Emerson! Speak of all that is in your mind. You have now an opportunity that may never come again."

There was a dead level in her voice that a little puzzled her husband.

"It is for you to speak," he answered. "I have put my interrogatories."

Unhappily, there was a shade of imperiousness in his voice.

" I never answer insulting interrogatories ; not even

from the man who calls himself my husband," replied Irene, haughtily.

"It may be best for you to answer," said Hartley. There was just the shadow of menace in his tones.

"Best!" The lip of Irene curled slightly. "On whose account, pray?"

"Best for each of us. Whatever affects one injuriously must affect both."

"Humph! So we are equals!" Irene tossed her head impatiently, and laughed a short, mocking laugh.

"Nothing of that, if you please!" was the husband's impatient retort. The sudden change in his wife's manner threw him off his guard.

"Nothing of what?" demanded Irene.

"Of that weak, silly nonsense. We have graver matters in hand for consideration now."

"Ah?" She threw up her eyebrows, then contracted them again with an angry severity.

"Irene," said Mr. Emerson, his voice falling into a calm but severe tone, "all this is but weakness and folly. I have heard things touching your good name -"

"And believe them," broke in Irene, with angry impatience.

"I have said nothing as to belief or disbelief. The fact is grave enough."

"And you have illustrated your faith in the slander - beautifully, becomingly, generously!"

"Irene!"

"Generously, as a man who knew his wife. Ah, well!" This last ejaculation was made almost lightly, but it involved great bitterness of spirit.

"Do not speak any longer after this fashion," said Hartley, with considerable irritation of manner; "it doesn't suit my present temper. I want something in a very different spirit. The matter is of too serious import. So pray lay aside your trifling. I came to you as I had a right to come, and made inquiries touching your associations when not in my company. Your answers are not satisfactory, but tend rather to con -"

"Sir!" Irene interrupted him in a stern, deep voice, which came so suddenly that the word remained unspoken. Then, raising her finger in a warning manner, she said with menace,

"Beware!"

For some moments they stood looking at each other, more like two animals at bay than husband and wife.

"Touching my associations when not in your company?" said Irene at length, repeating his language slowly.

"Yes," answered the husband.

"Touching, my associations? Well, Mr. Emerson - so far, I say well." She was collected in manner and her voice steady. "But what touching your associations when not in *my* company?"

The very novelty of this interrogation caused Emerson to start and change color.

"Ha!" The blood leaped to the forehead of Irene, and her eyes, dilating suddenly, almost glared upon the face of her husband.

"*Well, sir?*" Irene drew her slender form to its utmost height. There was an impatient, demanding tone in her voice. "Speak!" she added, without change of manner. "What touching *your* associations when not in *my* company? As a wife, I have some interest in this matter. Away from home often until the brief hours, have I no right to put the question - where and with whom? It would seem so if we are equal. But if I am the slave and dependant - the creature of your will and pleasure - why, that alters the case!"

"Have you done?"

Emerson was recovering from his surprise, but not gaining clear sight or prudent self-possession.

"You have not answered," said Irene, looking coldly, but with glittering eyes, into his face. "Come! If there is to be a mutual relation of acts and associations outside of this our home, let us begin. Sit down, Hartley, and compose yourself. You are the man, and claim precedence. I yield the prerogative. So let me have your confession. After you have ended I will give as faithful a narrative as if on my death-bed. What more can you ask? There now, lead the way!"

This coolness, which but thinly veiled a contemptuous air, irritated Hartley almost beyond the bounds of decent self-control.

"Bravely carried off! Well acted!" he retorted with a sneer.

"You do not accept the proposal," said Irene, growing a little sterner of aspect. "Very well. I scarcely hoped that you would meet me on this even ground. Why should I have hoped it? Were the antecedents encouraging? No! But I am sorry. Ah, well! Husbands are free to go and come at their own sweet will - to associate with anybody and everybody. But wives - oh dear!"

She tossed her head in a wild, scornful way, as if on the verge of being swept from her feet by some whirlwind of passion.

"And so," said her husband, after a long silence, "you do not choose to answer my questions as to Major Willard?"

That was unwisely pressed. In her heart of hearts Irene loathed this man. His name was an offence to her. Never, since the night he had forced himself into her carriage, had she even looked into his face. If he appeared in the room where she happened to be, she did not permit her eyes to rest upon his detested countenance. If he drew near to her, she did not seem to notice his presence. If he spoke to her, as he had ventured several times to do, she paid no regard to him whatever. So far as any response or manifestation of feeling on her part was concerned, it was as if his voice had not reached her ears. The very thought of this man was a foul thing in her mind. No wonder that the repeated reference by her husband was felt as a stinging insult.

"If you dare to mention that name again in connection with mine," she said, turning almost fiercely upon him, "I will -"

She caught the words and held them back in the silence of her wildly reeling thoughts.

"Say on!"

Emerson was cool, but not sane. It was madness to press his excited young wife now. Had he lost sense and discrimination? Could he not see, in her strong, womanly indignation, the signs of innocence? Fool! fool! to thrust sharply at her now!

"My father!" came in a sudden gush of strong feeling from the lips of Irene, as the thought of him whose name was thus ejaculated came into her mind. She struck her hands together, and stood like one in wild bewilderment. "My father!" she added, almost mournfully; "oh, that I had never left you!"

"It would have been better for you and better for me." No, he was not sane, else would no such words have fallen from his lips.

Irene, with a slight start and a slight change in the expression of her countenance, looked up at her husband:

"You think so?" Emerson was a little surprised at the way in which Irene put this interrogation. He looked for a different reply.

"I have said it," was his cold answer.

"Well." She said no more, but looked down and sat thinking for the space of more than a minute.

"I will go back to Ivy Cliff." She looked up, with something strange in the expression of her face. It was a blank, unfeeling, almost unmeaning expression.

"Well." It was Emerson's only response.

"Well; and that is all?" Her tones were so chilling that they came over the spirit of her husband like the low waves of an icy wind.

"No, that is not all." What evil spirit was blinding his perceptions? What evil influence pressing him on to the brink of ruin?

"Say on." How strangely cold and calm she remained! "Say on," she repeated. Was there none to warn him of danger?

"If you go a third time to your father - " He paused.

"Well?" There was not a quiver in her low, clear, icy tone.

"You must do it with your eyes open, and in full view of the consequences."

"What are the consequences?"

Beware, rash man! Put a seal on your lips! Do not let

the thought so sternly held find even a shadow of utterance!

"Speak, Hartley Emerson. What are the consequences?"

"You cannot return!" It was said without a quiver of feeling.

"Well." She looked at him with an unchanged countenance, steadily, coldly, piercingly.

"I have said the words, Irene; and they are no idle utterances. Twice you have left me, but you cannot do it a third time and leave a way open between us. Go, then, if you will; but, if we part here, it must be for ever!"

The eyes of Irene dropped slowly. There was a slight change in the expression of her face. Her hands moved one within the other nervously.

For ever! The words are rarely uttered without leaving on the mind a shade of thought. For ever! They brought more than a simple shadow to the mind of Irene. A sudden darkness fell upon her soul, and for a little while she groped about like one who had lost her way. But her husband's threat of consequences, his cold, imperious manner, his assumed superiority, all acted as sharp spurs to pride, and she stood up, strong again, in full mental stature, with every power of her being in full force for action and endurance.

"I go." There was no sign of weakness in her voice. She had raised her eyes from the floor and turned them full upon her husband. Her face was not so pale as it had been a little while before. Warmth had come back to the delicate skin, flushing it with beauty. She did not stand before him an impersonation of anger, dislike or rebellion. There was not a repulsive attitude or expression; no flashing of the eyes, nor even the cold, diamond glitter seen a little while before. Slowly turning away, she left the room; but, to her husband, she seemed still standing there, a lovely vision. There had fallen, in that instant of time, a sunbeam which fixed the image upon his memory in imperishable colors. What though he parted company here with the vital form, that effigy would be, through all time, his inseparable companion!

"Gone!" Hartley Emerson held his breath as the word came into mental utterance. There was a motion of regret in his heart; a wish that he had not spoken quite so sternly - that he had kept back a part of the hard saying. But it was too late now. He could not, after all that had just passed between them - after she had refused to answer his questions touching Major Willard - make any concessions. Come what would, there was to be no retracing of steps now.

"And it may be as well," said he, rallying himself, "that we part here. Our experiment has proved a sad failure. We grow colder and more repellant each day, instead of drawing closer together and becoming more lovingly assimilated. It is not good - this life - for either of us. We struggle in our bonds and hurt each other. Better apart! better apart! Moreover" - his face darkened - "she has fallen into dangerous companionship, and will not be advised or governed. I have heard her name fall lightly from lips that cannot utter a woman's name without leaving it soiled. She is pure now - pure as snow. I have not a shadow of suspicion, though I pressed her close. But this contact is bad; she is breathing an impure atmosphere; she is assorting with some who are sensual and evil-minded, though she will not believe the truth. Mrs. Lloyd! Gracious heavens! My wife the intimate companion of that woman! Seen with her in Broadway! A constant visitor at my house! This, and I knew it not!"

Emerson grew deeply agitated as he rehearsed these things. It was after midnight when he retired. He did not go to his wife's apartment, but passed to a room in the story above that in which he usually slept.

Day was abroad when Emerson awoke the next morning, and the sun shining from an angle that showed him to be nearly two hours above the horizon. It was late for Mr. Emerson. Rising hurriedly, and in some confusion of thought, he went down stairs. His mind, as the events of the last evening began to adjust themselves, felt an increasing sense of oppression. How was he to meet Irene? or was he to meet her again? Had she relented? Had a night of sober reflection wrought any change? Would she take the step he had warned her as a fatal one?

With such questions crowding upon him, Hartley Emerson went down stairs. In passing their chamber-door he saw that it stood wide open, and that Irene was not there. He descended to the parlors and to the sitting-room, but did not find her. The bell announced breakfast; he might find her at the table. No - she was not at her usual place when the morning meal was served.

"Where is Mrs. Emerson?" he asked of the waiter.

"I have not seen her," was replied.

Mr. Emerson turned away and went up to their chambers. His footsteps had a desolate, echoing sound to his ears, as he bent his way thither. He looked through the front and then through the back chamber, and even called, faintly, the name of his wife. But all was still as death. Now a small envelope caught his eye, resting on a casket in which Irene had kept her jewelry. He lifted it, and saw his name inscribed thereon. The handwriting was not strange. He broke the seal and read these few words:

"I have gone. IRENE."

The narrow piece of tinted paper on which this was written dropped from his nerveless fingers, and he stood for some moments still as if death-stricken, and rigid as stone.

"Well," he said audibly, at length, stepping across the floor, "and so the end has come!"

He moved to the full length of the chamber and then stood still - turned, in a little while, and walked slowly back across the floor - stood still again, his face bent down, his lips closely shut, his finger-ends gripped into the palms.

"Gone!" He tried to shake himself free of the partial stupor which had fallen upon him. "Gone!" he repeated. "And so this calamity is upon us! She has dared the fatal leap! has spoken the irrevocable decree! God help us both, for both have need of help; I and she, but she most. God help her to bear the burden she has lifted to her weak shoulders; she will find it a

T. S. Arthur

match for her strength. I shall go into the world and bury myself in its cares and duties - shall find, at least, in the long days a compensation in work - earnest, absorbing, exciting work. But she? Poor Irene! The days and nights will be to her equally desolate. Poor Irene! Poor Irene!"

CHAPTER XVIII.

YOUNG, BUT WISE.

THE night had passed wearily for Mr. Delancy, broken by fitful dreams, in which the image of his daughter was always present - dreams that he could trace to no thoughts or impressions of the day before; and he arose unrefreshed, and with a vague sense of trouble in his heart, lying there like a weight which no involuntary deep inspirations would lessen or remove. No June day ever opened in fresher beauty than did this one, just four years since the actors in our drama came smiling before us, in the flush of youth and hope and confidence in the far-off future. The warmth of early summer had sent the nourishing sap to every delicate twig and softly expanding leaf until, full foliaged, the trees around Ivy Cliff stood in kingly attire, lifting themselves up grandly in the sunlight which flooded their gently-waving tops in waves of golden glory. The air was soft and of crystal clearness; and the lungs drank it in as if the draught were ethereal nectar.

On such a morning in June, after a night of broken and unrefreshing sleep, Mr. Delancy walked forth, with that strange pressure on his heart which he had been vainly endeavoring to push aside since the singing birds awoke him, in the faint auroral dawn, with their joyous welcome to the coming day. He drew in long draughts of the delicious air; expanded his chest; moved briskly through the garden; threw his arms about to hurry the sluggish flow of blood in his veins; looked with constrained admiration on the splendid landscape that stretched far and near in the sweep of his vision; but all to no purpose. The hand still lay heavy upon his heart; he could not get it removed.

Returning to the house, feeling more uncomfortable for this fruitless effort to rise above what he tried to call an unhealthy depression of spirits consequent on some morbid state of the body, Mr. Delancy was entering the library, when a fresh young face greeted him with light and smiles.

"Good-morning, Rose," said the old gentleman, as his face brightened in the glow of the young girl's happy countenance. "I am glad to see you;" and he took her hand and held it tightly.

"Good-morning, Mr. Delancy. When did you hear from Irene?"

"Ten days ago."

"She was well?"

"Oh yes. Sit down, Rose; there." And Mr. Delancy drew a chair before the sofa for his young visitor, and took a seat facing her.

"I haven't had a letter from her in six months," said Rose, a sober hue falling on her countenance.

"I don't think she is quite thoughtful enough of her old friends."

"And too thoughtful, it may be, of new ones," replied Mr. Delancy, his voice a little depressed from the cheerful tone in which he had welcomed his young visitor.

"These new friends are not always the best friends, Mr. Delancy."

"No, Rose. For my part, I wouldn't give one old friend, whose heart I had proved, for a dozen untried new ones."

"Nor I, Mr. Delancy. I love Irene. I have always loved her. You know we were children together."

"Yes, dear, I know all that; and I'm not pleased with her for treating you with so much neglect, and all for a set of - "

Mr. Delancy checked himself.

"Irene," said Miss Carman, whom the reader will remember as one of Mrs. Emerson's bridemaids, "has been a little unfortunate in her New York friends. I'm afraid of these strong-minded women, as they are called, among whom she has fallen."

"I detest them!" replied Mr. Delancy, with suddenly aroused feelings. "They have done my child more harm than they will ever do good in the world by way of atonement. She is not my daughter of old."

"I found her greatly changed at our last meeting," said Rose. "Full of vague plans of reforms and social reorganizations, and impatient of opposition, or even mild argument, against her favorite ideas."

"She has lost her way," sighed the old man, in a low, sad voice, "and I'm afraid it will take her a long, long time to get back again to the old true paths, and that the road will be through deep suffering. I dreamed about her all night, Rose, and the shadow of my dreams is upon me still. It is foolish, I know, but I cannot get my heart again into the sunlight."

And Rose had been dreaming troubled dreams of her old friend, also; and it was because of the pressure that lay upon her feelings that she had come over to Ivy Cliff this morning to ask if Mr. Delancy had heard from Irene. She did not, however, speak of this, for she saw that he was in an unhappy state on account of his daughter.

"Dreams are but shadows," she said, forcing a smile to her lips and eyes.

"Yes - yes." The old man responded with an abstracted air. "Yes; they are only shadows. But, my dear, was there ever a shadow without a substance?"

"Not in the outside world of nature. Dreams are unreal things - the fantastic images of a brain where reason sleeps."

"There have been dreams that came as warnings, Rose."

"And a thousand, for every one of these, that signified nothing."

"True. But I cannot rise out of these shadows. They lie too heavily on my spirit. You must bear with me, Rose. Thank you for coming over to see me; but I cannot make your visit a pleasant one, and you must leave me when you grow weary of the old man's company."

"Don't talk so, Mr. Delancy. I'm glad I came over. I meant this only for a call; but as you are in such poor spirits I must stay a while and cheer you up."

"You are a good girl," said Mr. Delancy, taking the hand of Rose, "and I am vexed that Irene should neglect you for the false friends who are leading her mind astray. But never mind, dear; she will see her error one of these days, and learn to prize true hearts."

"Is she going to spend much of her time at Ivy Cliff this summer?" asked Rose.

"She is coming up in July to stay three or four weeks."

"Ah? I'm pleased to hear you say so. I shall then revive old-time memories in her heart."

"God grant that it may be so!" Rose half started at the solemn tone in which Mr. Delancy spoke. What could be the meaning of his strangely troubled manner? Was anything seriously wrong with Irene? She remembered the confusion into which her impulsive conduct had thrown the wedding-party; and there was a vague rumor afloat that Irene had left her husband a few months afterward and returned to Ivy Cliff. But she had always discredited this rumor. Of her life in New York she knew but little as to particulars. That it was not making of her a truer, better, happier woman, nor a truer, better, happier wife, observation had long ago told her.

"There is a broad foundation of good principles in her

character," said Miss Carman, "and this gives occasion for hope in the future. She will not go far astray, with her wily enticers, who have only stimulated and given direction, for a time, to her undisciplined impulses. You know how impatient she has always been under control - how restively her spirit has chafed itself when a restraining hand was laid upon her. But there are real things in life of too serious import to be set aside for idle fancies, such as her new friends have dignified with imposing names - real things, that take hold upon the solid earth like anchors, and hold the vessel firm amid wildly rushing currents."

"Yes, Rose, I know all that," replied Mr. Delancy. "I have hope in the future of Irene; but I shudder in heart to think of the rough, thorny, desolate ways through which she may have to pass with bleeding feet before she reaches that serene future. Ah! if I could save my child from the pain she seems resolute on plucking down and wearing in her heart!"

"Your dreams have made you gloomy, Mr. Delancy," said Rose, forcing a smile to her sweet young face. "Come now, let us be more hopeful. Irene has a good husband. A little too much like her in some things, but growing manlier and broader in mental grasp, if I have read him aright. He understands Irene, and, what is more, loves her deeply. I have watched them closely."

"So have I." The voice of Mr. Delancy was not so hopeful as that of his companion.

"Still looking on the darker side." She smiled again.

"Ah, Rose, my wise young friend," said Mr. Delancy, "to whom I speak my thoughts with a freedom that surprises even myself, a father's eyes read many signs that have no meaning for others."

"And many read them, through fond suspicion, wrong," replied Rose.

"Well - yes - that may be." He spoke in partial abstraction, yet doubtfully.

"I must look through your garden," said the young lady, rising; "you know how I love flowers."

"Not much yet to hold your admiration," replied Mr. Delancy, rising also. "June gives us wide green carpets and magnificent draperies of the same deep color, but her red and golden broideries are few; it is the hand of July that throws them in with rich profusion."

"But June flowers are sweetest and dearest - tender nurslings of the summer, first-born of her love," said Rose, as they stepped out into the portico. "It may be that the eye gets sated with beauty, as nature grows lavish of her gifts; but the first white and red petals that unfold themselves have a more delicate perfume - seem made of purer elements and more wonderful in perfection - than their later sisters. Is it not so?"

"If it only appears so it is all the same as if real," replied Mr. Delancy, smiling.

"How?"

"It is real to you. What more could you have? Not more enjoyment of summer's gifts of beauty and sweetness."

"No; perhaps not."

Rose let her eyes fall to the ground, and remained silent.

"Things are real to us as we see them; not always as they are," said Mr. Delancy.

"And this is true of life?"

"Yes, child. It is in life that we create for ourselves real things out of what to some are airy nothings. Real things, against which we often bruise or maim ourselves, while to others they are as intangible as shadows."

"I never thought of that," said Rose.

"It is true."

"Yes, I see it. Imaginary evils we thus make real things, and hurt ourselves by contact, as, maybe, you have done this morning, Mr. Delancy."

"Yes - yes. And false ideas of things which are unrealities in the abstract - for only what is true has actual substance - become real to the perverted understanding. Ah, child, there are strange contradictions and deep problems in life for each of us to solve."

"But, God helping us, we may always reach the true solution," said Rose Carman, lifting a bright, confident face to that of her companion.

"That was spoken well, my child," returned Mr. Delancy, with a new life in his voice; "and without

Him we can never be certain of our way."

"Never - never." There was a tender, trusting solemnity in the voice of Rose.

"Young, but wise," said Mr. Delancy.

"No! Young, but not wise. I cannot see the way plain before me for a single week, Mr. Delancy. For a week? No, not for a day!"

"Who does?" asked the old man.

"Some."

"None. There are many who walk onward with erect heads and confident bearing. They are sure of their way, and smile if one whisper a caution as to the ground upon which they step so fearlessly. But they soon get astray or into pitfalls. God keeping and guiding us, Rose, we may find our way safely through this world. But we will soon lose ourselves if we trust in our own wisdom."

Thus they talked - that old man and gentle-hearted girl - as they moved about the garden-walks, every new flower, or leaf, or opening bud they paused to admire or examine, suggesting themes for wiser words than usually pass between one so old and one so young. At Mr. Delancy's earnest request, Rose stayed to dinner, the waiting-man being tent to her father's, not far distant, to take word that she would not be at home until in the afternoon.

CHAPTER XIX.

THE SHIPWRECKED LIFE.

OFTEN, during that morning, did the name of Irene come to their lips, for the thought of her was all the while present to both.

"You must win her heart back again, Rose," said Mr. Delancy. "I will lure her to Ivy Cliff often this summer, and keep her here as long as possible each time. You will then be much together." They had risen from the dinner-table and were entering the library.

"Things rarely come out as we plan them," answered Rose. "But I love Irene truly, and will make my own place in her heart again, if she will give me the key of entrance."

"You must find the key, Rose."

Miss Carman smiled.

"I said if she would give it to me."

"She does not carry the key that opens the door for you," replied Mr. Delancy. "If you do not know where it lies, search for it in the secret places of your own mind, and it will be found, God helping you, Rose."

Mr. Delancy looked at her significantly.

"God helping me," she answered, with a reverent sinking of her voice, "I will find the key."

"Who is that?" said Mr. Delancy, in a tone of surprise, turning his face to the window.

Rose followed his eyes, but no one was visible.

"I saw, or thought I saw, a lady cross the portico this moment."

Both stood still, listening and expectant.

"It might have been fancy," said Mr. Delancy, drawing a deep breath.

Rose stepped to one of the library windows, and throwing it up, looked out upon the portico.

"There is no one," she remarked, coming back into the room.

"Could I have been so mistaken?"

Mr. Delancy looked bewildered.

Seeing that the impression was so strong on his mind, Miss Carman went out into the hall, and glanced from there into the parlor and dining-room.

"No one came in, Mr. Delancy," she said, on returning to the library.

"A mere impression," remarked the old man, soberly.

"Well, these impressions are often very singular. My face was partly turned to the window, so that I saw out, but not so distinctly as if both eyes had been in the range of vision. The form of a woman came to my sight as distinctly as if the presence had been real - the form of a woman going swiftly past the window."

"Did you recognize the form?"

It was some time before Mr. Delancy replied.

"Yes." He looked anxious.

"You thought of Irene?"

"I did."

"We have talked and thought of Irene so much to-day," said Rose, "that your thought of her has made you present to her mind with more than usual distinctness. Her thought of you has been more intent in consequence, and this has drawn her nearer. You saw her by an inward, not by an outward, vision. She is now present with you in spirit, though her body be many miles distant. These things often happen. They startle us by their strangeness, but are as much dependent on laws of the mind as bodily nearness is dependent on the laws of matter."

"You think so?" Mr. Delancy looked at his young companion curiously.

"Yes, I think so."

The old man shook his head. "Ingenious, but not satisfactory."

"You will admit," said Rose, "that as to our minds we may be present in any part of the world, and in an instant of time, though our bodies move not."

"Our thought may be," replied Mr. Delancy. "Or, in better words, the eyes of our minds may be; for it is the eyes that see objects," said Rose.

"Well; say the eyes of our minds, then."

"We cannot see objects in London, for instance, with our bodily eyes unless our bodies be in London?" resumed Rose.

"Of course not."

"Nor with our mental eyes, unless our spirits be there."

Mr. Delancy looked down thoughtfully.

"It must be true, then, that our thought of any one brings us present to that individual, and that such presence is often recognized."

"That is pushing the argument too far."

"I think not. Has it not often happened that suddenly the thought of an absent one came into your mind, and that you saw him or her for a moment or two almost as distinctly as if in bodily presence before you?"

"Yes. That has many times been the case."

"And you had not been thinking of that person, nor had there been any incident as a reminder?"

"I believe not."

"My explanation is, that this person from some cause had been led to think of you intently, and so came to you in spirit. There was actual presence, and you saw each other with the eyes of your minds."

"But, my wise reasoner," said Mr. Delancy, "it was the bodily form - with face, eyes, hands, feet and material garments - that was seen, not the spirit. If our spirits have eyes that see, why they can only see spiritual things."

"Has not a spirit a face, and hands, and feet?" asked Rose, with a confidence that caused the old man to look at her almost wonderingly.

"Not a face, and hands, and feet like these of mine," he answered.

"Yes, like them," she replied, "but of spiritual substance."

"Spiritual substance! That is a novel term. This is substance." And Mr. Delancy grasped the arm of a chair.

"No, that is material and unsubstantial," she calmly replied; "it is subject to change and decay. A hundred years from now and there may be no visible sign that it had ever been. But the soul is imperishable and immortal; the only thing about man that is really substantial. And now," she added, "for the faces of our spirits. What gives to our natural faces their form, beauty and expression? Is it not the soul-face within? Remove that by death, and all life, thought and feeling are gone from the stolid effigy. And so you see, Mr. Delancy, that our minds must be formed of spiritual substance, and that our bodies are but the outward material clothing which the soul puts on for action and use in this world of nature."

"Why, you are a young philosopher!" exclaimed Mr. Delancy, looking in wonder at his fair companion.

"No," she answered, with simplicity, "I talk with my father about these things, and it all seems very plain to me. I cannot see how any one can question what appears to me so plain. That the mind is substantial we see from this fact alone - it retains impressions longer than the body."

"You think so?"

"Take an instance," said Rose. "A boy is punished unjustly by a passionate teacher, who uses taunting words as well as smarting blows. Now the pain of these blows is gone in less than an hour, but the word-strokes received on his spirit hurt him, maybe, to the end of his mortal life. Is it not so? And if so, why? There must be substance to hold impressions so long."

"You silence, if you do not fully convince," replied Mr. Delancy. "I must dream over what you have said. And so your explanation is, that my thought of Irene has turned her thought to me, and thus we became really present?"

"Yes."

"And that I saw her just now by an inner, and not by an outer, sight?"

T. S. Arthur

"Yes."

"But why was the appearance an outward manifestation, so to speak?"

"Sight is in the mind, even natural sight. The eye does not go out to a tree, but the image of the tree comes to the eye, and thence is presented, in a wonderful and mysterious way, to the mind, which takes note of its form. The appearance is, that the soul looks out at the tree; but the fact is, the image of the tree comes to the brain, and is there seen. Now the brain may be impressed, and respond by natural vision, from an internal as well as from an external communication. We see this in cases of visual aberrations, the instances of which given in books, and clearly authenticated, are innumerable. Things are distinctly seen in a room which have no existence in nature; and the illusion is so perfect that it seems impossible for eyes to be mistaken."

"Well, well, child," said Mr. Delancy, "this is curious, and a little bewildering. Perhaps it is all just as you say about Irene; but I feel very heavy here;" and he laid his hand on his breast and sighed deeply.

At this moment the library door was pushed gently open, and the form of a woman stood in the presence of Mr. Delancy and Rose. She was dressed in a dark silk, but had on neither bonnet nor shawl. Both started; Mr. Delancy raised his hands and bent forward, gazing at her eagerly, his lips apart. The face of the woman was pale and haggard, yet familiar as the face of an old friend; but in it was something so strange and unnatural that for a moment or two it was not recognized.

"Father!" It was Irene. She advanced quietly and held but her hand.

"My daughter!" He caught the extended hand and kissed her, but she showed no emotion.

"Rose, dear, I am glad to see you." There was truth in the dead level tone with which "I am glad to see you" was spoken, and Rose, who perceived this, took her hand and kissed her. Both hands and lips were cold.

"What's the matter, Irene? Have you been sick?" asked Mr. Delancy, in a choking voice.

"No, father, I'm very well." You would never have recognized that voice as the voice of Irene.

"No, child, you are not well. What ails you? Why are you here in so strange a way and looking so strangely?"

"Do I look strangely?" There was a feeble effort to awaken a smile, which only gave her face a ghastly expression.

"Is Hartley with you?"

"No." Her voice was fuller and more emphatic as she uttered this word. She tried to look steadily at her father, but her eyes moved aside from the range of his vision.

For a little while there was a troubled silence with all. Rose had placed an arm around the waist of Irene and drawn her to the sofa, on which they were now sitting; Mr. Delancy stood before them. Gradually the cold, almost blank, expression of Irene's face changed and the old look came back.

"My daughter," said Mr. Delancy.

"Father" - Irene interrupted him - "I know what you are going to say. My sudden, unannounced appearance, at this time, needs explanation. I am glad dear Rose is here - my old, true friend" - and she leaned against Miss Carman - "I can trust her."

The arm of Rose tightened around the waist of Irene.

"Father" - the voice of Irene fell to a deep, solemn tone; there was no emphasis on one word more than on another; all was a dead level; yet the meaning was as full and the involved purpose as fixed as if her voice had run through the whole range of passionate intonation - "Father, I have come back to Ivy Cliff and to you, after having suffered shipwreck on the voyage of life. I went out rich, as I supposed, in heart-treasures; I come back poor. My gold was dross, and the sea has swallowed up even that miserable substitute for wealth. Hartley and I never truly loved each other, and the experiment of living together as husband and wife has proved a failure. We have not been happy; no, not from the beginning. We have not even been tolerant or forbearing toward each other. A steady alienation has been in progress day by day, week by week, and month by month, until no remedy is left but separation. That has been, at length, applied, and here I am! It is the third time that I have left him, and to both of us the act is final. He will not seek me, and I shall not return."

There had come a slight flush to the countenance of

Irene before she commenced speaking, but this retired again, and she looked deathly pale. No one answered her - only the arm of Rose tightened like a cord around the waist of her unhappy friend.

"Father," and now her voice fluttered a little, "for your sake I am most afflicted. I am strong enough to bear my fate - but you!"

There was a little sob - a strong suppression of feeling - and silence.

"Oh, Irene! my child! my child!" The old man covered his face with his hands, sobbed, and shook like a fluttering leaf. "I cannot bear this! It is too much for me!" and he staggered backward. Irene sprung forward and caught him in her arms. He would have fallen, but for this, to the floor. She stood clasping and kissing him wildly, until Rose came forward and led them both to the sofa.

Mr. Delancy did not rally from this shock. He leaned heavily against his daughter, and she felt a low tremor in his frame.

"Father!" She spoke tenderly, with her lips to his ear. "Dear father!"

But he did not reply.

"It is my life-discipline, father," she said; "I will be happier and better, no doubt, in the end for this severe trial. Dear father, do not let what is inevitable so break down your heart. You are my strong, brave, good father, and I shall need now more than ever, your sustaining arm. There was no help for this. It had to

T. S. Arthur

come, sooner or later. It is over now. The first bitterness is past. Let us be thankful for that, and gather up our strength for the future. Dear father! Speak to me!"

Mr. Delancy tried to rally himself, but he was too much broken down by the shock. He said a few words, in which there was scarcely any connection of ideas, and then, getting up from the sofa, walked about the room, turning one of his hands within the other in a distressed way.

"Oh dear, dear, dear!" he murmured to himself, in a feeble manner. "I have dreaded this, and prayed that it might not be. Such wretchedness and disgrace! Such wretchedness and disgrace! Had they no patience with each other - no forbearance - no love, that it must come to this? Dear! dear! dear! Poor child!"

Irene, with her white, wretched face, sat looking at him for some time, as he moved about, a picture of helpless misery; then, going to him again, she drew an arm around his neck and tried to comfort him. But there was no comfort in her words. What could *she* say to reach with a healing power the wound from which his very life-blood was pouring.

"Don't talk! don't talk!" he said, pushing Irene away, with slight impatience of manner. "I am heart-broken. Words are nothing!"

"Mr. Delancy," said Rose, now coming to his side, and laying a hand upon his arm, "you must not speak so to Irene. This is not like you."

There was a calmness of utterance and a firmness of

manner which had their right effect.

"How have I spoken, Rose, dear? What have I said?"
Mr. Delancy stopped and looked at Miss Carman in a
rebuked, confused way, laying his hand upon his
forehead at the same time.

"Not from yourself," answered Rose.

"Not from myself!" He repeated her words, as if his
thoughts were still in a maze. "Ah, child, this is dread-
ful!" he added. "I am not myself! Poor Irene! Poor
daughter! Poor father!"

And the old man lost himself again.

A look of fear now shadowed darkly the face of Irene,
and she glanced anxiously from her father's countenance to that of Rose. She did not read in the face of
her young friend much that gave assurance or comfort.

"Mr. Delancy," said Rose, with great earnestness of
manner, "Irene is in sore trouble. She has come to a
great crisis in her life. You are older and wiser than she
is, and must counsel and sustain her. Be calm, dear sir
- calm, clear-seeing, wise and considerate, as you have
always been."

"Calm - clear-seeing - wise." Mr. Delancy repeated the
words, as if endeavoring to grasp the rein of thought
and get possession of himself again.

"Wise to counsel and strong to sustain," said Rose.
"You must not fail us now."

"Thank you, my sweet young monitor," replied Mr.

Delancy, partially recovering himself; "it was the weakness of a moment. Irene," and he looked toward his daughter, "leave me with my own thoughts for a little while. Take her, Rose, to her own room, and God give you power to speak words of consolation; I have none."

Rose drew her arm within that of Irene, and said, "Come." But Irene lingered, looking tenderly and anxiously at her father.

"Go, my love." Mr. Delancy waved his hand.

"Father! dear father!" She moved a step toward him, while Rose held her back.

"I cannot help myself, father. The die is cast. Oh bear up with me! I will be to you a better daughter than I have ever been. My life shall be devoted to your happiness. In that I will find a compensation. All is not lost - all is not ruined. My heart is as pure as when I left you three years ago. I come back bleeding from my life-battle it is true, but not in mortal peril - wounded, but not unto death - cast down, but not destroyed."

All the muscles of Mr. Delancy's face quivered with suppressed feeling as he stood looking at his daughter, who, as she uttered the words, "cast down, but not destroyed," flung herself in wild abandonment on his breast.

CHAPTER XX.

THE PALSIED HEART.

THE shock to Mr. Delancy was a fearful one, coming as it did on a troubled, foreboding state of mind; and reason lost for a little while her firm grasp on the rein of government. If the old man could have seen a ray of hope in the case it would have been different. But from the manner and language of his daughter it was plain that the dreaded evil had found them; and the certainty of this falling suddenly, struck him as with a heavy blow.

For several days he was like one who had been stunned. All that afternoon on which his daughter returned to Ivy Cliff he moved about in a bewildered way, and by his questions and remarks showed an incoherence of thought that filled the heart of Irene with alarm.

On the next morning, when she met him at the breakfast-table, he smiled on her in his old affectionate way. As she kissed him, she said,

"I hope you slept well last night, father?"

A slight change was visible in his face.

"I slept soundly enough," he replied, "but my dreams were not agreeable."

Then he looked at her with a slight closing of the brows and a questioning look in his eyes.

They sat down, Irene taking her old place at the table. As she poured out her father's coffee, he said, smiling,

"It is pleasant to have you sitting there, daughter."

"Is it?"

Irene was troubled by this old manner of her father. Could he have forgotten why she was there?

"Yes, it is pleasant," he replied, and then his eye dropped in a thoughtful way.

"I think, sometimes, that your attractive New York friends have made you neglectful of your lonely old father. You don't come to see him as often as you did a year ago."

Mr. Delancy said this with simple earnestness.

"They shall not keep me from you any more, dear father," replied Irene, meeting his humor, yet heart-appalled at the same time with this evidence that his mind was wandering from the truth.

"I don't think them safe friends," added Mr. Delancy, with seriousness.

"Perhaps not," replied Irene.

"Ah! I'm glad to hear you say so. Now, you have one true, safe friend. I wish you loved her better than you do."

"What is her name?"

"Rose Carman," said Mr. Delancy, with a slight hesitation of manner, as if he feared repulsion on the part of his daughter.

"I love Rose, dearly; she is the best of girls; and I know her to be a true friend," replied Irene.

"Spoken like my own daughter!" said the old man with a brightening countenance. "You must not neglect her any more. Why, she told me you hadn't written to her in six months. Now, that isn't right. Never go past old, true friends for the sake of new, and maybe false ones. No - no. Rose is hurt; you must write to her often - every week."

Irene could not answer. Her heart was beating wildly. What could this mean? Had reason fled? But she struggled hard to preserve a calm exterior.

"Will Hartley be up to-day?"

Irene tried to say "No," but could not find utterance.

Mr. Delancy looked at her curiously, and now in a slightly troubled way. Then he let his eyes fall, and sat holding his cup like one who was turning perplexed thoughts in his mind.

"You are not well this morning, father," said Irene, speaking only because silence was too oppressive for endurance.

"I don't know; perhaps I'm not very well; and Mr. Delancy looked across the table at his daughter very earnestly. "I had bad dreams all last night, and they seem to have got mixed up in my thoughts with real things. How is it? When did you come up from New York? Don't smile at me. But really I can't think."

"I came yesterday," said Irene, as calmly as she could speak.

"Yesterday!" He looked at her with a quickly changing face.

"Yes, father, I came up yesterday."

"And Rose was here?"

"Yes."

Mr. Delancy's eyes fell again, and he sat very still.

"Hartley will not be here to-day?"

Mr. Delancy did not look up as he asked this question.

"No, father."

"Nor to-morrow?"

"I think not."

A sigh quivered on the old man's lips.

"Nor the day after that?"

"He did not say when he was coming," replied Irene, evasively.

"Did not say when? Did not say when?" Mr. Delancy repeated the sentence two or three times, evidently trying all the while to recall something which had faded from his memory.

"Don't worry yourself about Hartley," said Irene, forcing herself to pronounce a name that seemed like fire on her lips. "Isn't it enough that I am here?"

"No, it is not enough." And her father put his hand to his forehead and looked upward in an earnest, searching manner.

What could Irene say? What could she do? The mind of her father was groping about in the dark, and she was every moment in dread lest he should discover the truth and get farther astray from the shock.

No food was taken by either Mr. Delancy or his daughter. The former grew more entangled in his thoughts, and finally arose from the table, saying, in a half-apologetic way,

"I don't know what ails me this morning."

"Where are you going?" asked Irene, rising at the same time.

"Nowhere in particular. The air is close here - I'll sit a while in the portico," he answered, and throwing open one of the windows he stepped outside. Irene followed him.

"How beautiful!" said Mr. Delancy, as he sat down and turned his eyes upon the attractive landscape. Irene did not trust her voice in reply.

"Now go in and finish your breakfast, child. I feel better; I don't know what came over me." He added the last sentence in an undertone.

Irene returned into the house, but not to resume her place at the table. Her mind was in an agony of dread. She had reached the dining-room, and was about to ring for a servant, when she heard her name called by her father. Running back quickly to the portico, she found him standing in the attitude of one who had been suddenly startled; his face all alive with question and suspense.

"Oh, yes! yes! I thought you were here this moment! And so it's all true?" he said, in a quick, troubled way.

"True? What is true, father?" asked Irene, as she paused before him.

"True, what you told me yesterday."

She did not answer.

"You have left your husband?" He looked soberly into her face.

"I have, father." She thought it best to use no evasion.

He groaned, sat down in the chair from which he had arisen, and let his head fall upon his bosom.

" Father ! " Irene kneeled before him and clasped his

hands. "Father! dear father!"

He laid a hand on her head, and smoothed her hair in a caressing manner.

"Poor child! poor daughter!" he said, in a fond, pitying voice, "don't take it so to heart. Your old father loves you still."

She could not stay the wild rush of feeling that was overmastering her. Passionate sobs heaved her breast, and tears came raining from her eyes.

"Now, don't, Irene! Don't take on so, daughter! I love you still, and we will be happy here, as in other days."

"Yes, father," said Irene, holding down her head and calming her voice, "we will be happy here, as in the dear old time. Oh we will be very happy together. I won't leave you any more."

"I wish you had never left me," he answered, mournfully; "I was always afraid of this - always afraid. But don't let it break your heart; I'm all the same; nothing will ever turn me against you. I hope he hasn't been very unkind to you?" His voice grew a little severe.

"We wont say anything against him," replied Irene, trying to understand exactly her father's state of mind and accommodate herself thereto. "Forgive and forget is the wisest rule always."

"Yes, dear, that's it. Forgive and forget - forgive and forget. There's nothing like it in this world. I'm glad to hear you talk so."

The mind of Mr. Delancy did not again wander from the truth. But the shock received when it first came upon him with stunning force had taken away his keen perception of the calamity. He was sad, troubled and restless, and talked a great deal about the unhappy position of his daughter - sometimes in a way that indicated much incoherence of thought. To this state succeeded one of almost total silence, and he would sit for hours, if not aroused from reverie and inaction by his daughter, in apparent dreamy listlessness. His conversation, when he did talk on any subject, showed, however, that his mind had regained its old clearness.

On the third day after Irene's arrival at Ivy Cliff, her trunks came up from New York. She had packed them on the night before leaving her husband's house, and marked them with her name and that of her father's residence. No letter or message accompanied them. She did not expect nor desire any communication, and was not therefore disappointed, but rather relieved from what would have only proved a cause of disturbance. All angry feelings toward her husband had subsided; but no tender impulses moved in her heart, nor did the feeblest thought of reconciliation breathe over the surface of her mind. She had been in bonds; now the fetters were cast off, and she loved freedom too well to bend her neck again to the yoke.

No tender impulses moved, we have said, in her heart, for it lay like a palsied thing, dead in her bosom - dead, we mean, so far as the wife was concerned. It was not so palsied on that fatal evening when the last strife with her husband closed. But in the agony that followed there came, in mercy, a cold paralysis; and now toward Hartley Emerson her feelings were as calm as the surface of a frozen lake.

And how was it with the deserted husband? Stern and unyielding also. The past year had been marked by so little of mutual tenderness, there had been so few passages of love between them - green spots in the desert of their lives - that memory brought hardly a relic from the past over which the heart could brood. For the sake of worldly appearances, Emerson most regretted the unhappy event. Next, his trouble was for Irene and her father, but most for Irene.

"Willful, wayward one!" he said many, many times. "You, of all, will suffer most. No woman can take a step like this without drinking of pain to the bitterest dregs. If you can hide the anguish, well. But I fear the trial will be too hard for you - the burden too heavy. Poor, mistaken one!"

For a month the household arrangements of Mr. Emerson continued as when Irene left him. He did not intermit for a day or an hour his business duties, and came home regularly at his usual times - always, it must be said, with a feeble expectation of meeting his wife in her old places; we do not say desire, but simply expectation. If she had returned, well. He would not have repulsed, nor would he have received her with strong indications of pleasure. But a month went by, and she did not return nor send him any word. Beyond the brief "I have gone," there had come from her no sign.

Two months elapsed, and then Mr. Emerson dismissed the servants and shut up the house, but he neither removed nor sold the furniture; that remained as it was for nearly a year, when he ordered a sale by auction and closed the establishment.

T. S. Arthur

Hartley Emerson, under the influence of business and domestic trouble, matured rapidly, and became grave, silent and reflective beyond men of his years. Companionable he was by nature, and during the last year that Irene was with him, failing to receive social sympathy at home, he had joined a club of young men, whose association was based on a declared ambition for literary excellence. From this club he withdrew himself; it did not meet the wants of his higher nature, but offered much that stimulated the grosser appetites and passions. Now he gave himself up to earnest self-improvement, and found in the higher and wider range of thought which came as the result a partial compensation for what he had lost. But he was not happy; far, very far from it. And there were seasons when the past came back upon him in such a flood that all the barriers of indifference which he had raised for self-protection were swept away, and he had to build them up again in sadness of spirit. So the time wore on with him, and troubled life-experiences were doing their work upon his character.

CHAPTER XXI.

THE IRREVOCABLE DECREE.

IT is two years since the day of separation between Irene and her husband. Just two years. And she is sitting in the portico at Ivy Cliff with her father, looking down upon the river that lies gleaming in sunshine - not thinking of the river, however, nor of anything in nature.

They are silent and still - very still, as if sleep had locked their senses. He is thin and wasted as from long sickness, and she looks older by ten years. There is no fine bloom on her cheeks, from which the fullness of youth has departed.

It is a warm June day, the softest, balmiest, brightest day the year has given. The air comes laden with delicate odors and thrilling with bird melodies, and, turn the eye as it will, there is a feast of beauty.

Yet, the odors are not perceived, nor the music heard, nor the beauty seen by that musing old man and his silent daughter. Their thoughts are not in the present, but far back in the unhappy past, the memories of which, awakened by the scene and season, have come flowing in a strong tide upon them.

T. S. Arthur

Two years! They have left the prints of their heavy feet upon the life of Irene, and the deep marks will never be wholly obliterated. She were less than human if this were not so. Two years! Yet, not once in that long, heart-aching time had she for a single moment looked backward in weakness. Sternly holding to her act as right, she strengthened herself in suffering, and bore her pain as if it were a decree of fate. There was no anger in her heart, nor anything of hardness toward her husband. But there was no love, nor tender yearning for conjunction - at least, nothing recognized as such in her own consciousness.

Not since the days Irene left the house of her husband had she heard from him directly; and only two or three times indirectly. She had never visited the city since her flight therefrom, and all her pleasant and strongly influencing associations there were, in consequence, at an end. Once her very dear friend Mrs. Talbot came up to sympathize with and strengthen her in the fiery trial through which she was passing. She found Irene's truer friend, Rosa Carman, with her; and Rose did not leave them alone for a moment at a time. All sentiments that she regarded as hurtful to Irene in her present state of mind she met with her calm, conclusive mode of reasoning, that took away the specious force of the sophist's dogmas. But her influence was chiefly used in the repression of unprofitable themes, and the introduction of such as tended to tranquilize the feelings, and turn the thoughts of her friend away from the trouble that was lying upon her soul like a suffocating nightmare. Mrs. Talbot was not pleased with her visit, and did not come again. But she wrote several times. The tone of her letters was not, however, pleasant to Irene, who was disturbed by it, and more bewildered than enlightened by the sentiments that were announced with oracular vagueness. These letters were read to Miss Carman, on whom Irene was beginning to lean with increasing confidence. Rose did not fail to expose their weakness or fallacy in such clear light that Irene, though she tried to shut her eyes against the truth presented by Rose, could not help seeing it. Her replies were not, under these circumstances, very satisfactory, for she was unable to speak in a free, assenting, confiding spirit. The consequence was natural. Mrs. Talbot ceased to write, and Irene did not regret the broken correspondence. Once Mrs. Lloyd wrote. When Irene broke the seal and let her eyes rest upon the signature, a shudder of repulsion ran through her frame, and the letter dropped from her hands to the floor. As if possessed by a spirit whose influence over her she could not control, she caught up the unread sheet and threw it into the fire. As the flames seized upon and consumed it, she drew a long breath and murmured,

"So perish the memory of our acquaintance!"

Almost a dead letter of suffering had been those two years. There are no events to record, and but little progress to state. Yes, there had been a dead level of suffering - a palsied condition of heart and mind; a period of almost sluggish endurance, in which pride and an indomitable will gave strength to bear.

Mr. Delancy and his daughter were sitting, as we have seen, on that sweet June day, in silent abstraction of thought, when the serving-man, who had been to the village, stepped into the portico and handed Irene a letter. The sight of it caused her heart to leap and the blood to crimson suddenly her face. It was not an ordinary letter - one in such a shape had never come to her hand before.

"What is that?" asked her father, coming back as it were to life.

"I don't know," she answered, with an effort to appear indifferent.

Mr. Delancy looked at his daughter with a perplexed manner, and then let his eyes fall upon the legal envelope in her hand, on which a large red seal was impressed.

Rising in a quiet way, Irene left the portico with slow steps; but no sooner was she beyond her father's observation than she moved toward her chamber with winged feet.

"Bless me, Miss Irene!" exclaimed Margaret, who met her on the stairs, "what has happened?"

But Irene swept by her without a response, and, entering her room, shut the door and locked it. Margaret stood a moment irresolute, and then, going back to her young lady's chamber, knocked for admission. There was no answer to her summons, and she knocked again.

"Who is it?"

She hardly knew the voice.

"It is Margaret. Can't I come in?"

"Not now," was answered.

"What's the matter, Miss Irene?"

"Nothing, Margaret. I wish to be alone now."

"Something has happened, though, or you'd never look just like that," said Margaret to herself, as she went slowly down stairs. "Oh dear, dear! Poor child! there's nothing but trouble for her in this world."

It was some minutes before Irene found courage to break the imposing seal and look at the communication within. She guessed at the contents, and was not wrong. They informed her, in legal phrase, that her husband had filed an application for a divorce on the ground of desertion, and gave notice that any resistance to this application must be on file on or before a certain date.

The only visible sign of feeling that responded to this announcement was a deadly paleness and a slight, nervous crushing of the paper in her hands. Moveless as a thing inanimate, she sat with fixed, dreamy eyes for a long, long time.

A divorce! She had looked for this daily for more than a year, and often wondered at her husband's tardiness. Had she desired it? Ah, that is the probing question. Had she desired an act of law to push them fully asunder - to make the separation plenary in all respects? No. She did not really wish for the irrevocable sundering decree.

Since her return to her father's house, the whole life of Irene had been marked by great circumspection. The trial through which she had passed was enough to sober her mind and turn her thoughts in some new directions; and this result had followed. Pride, self-will and impatience of control found no longer any spur to reactive life, and so her interest in woman's rights, social reforms and all their concomitants died away, for lack of a personal bearing. At first there had been warm arguments with Miss Carman on these subjects, but these grew gradually less earnest, and were finally avoided by both, as not only unprofitable, but distasteful. Gradually this wise and true friend had quickened in the mind of Irene an interest in things out of herself. There are in every neighborhood objects to awaken our sympathies, if we will only look at and think of them. "The poor ye have always with you." Not the physically poor only, but, in larger numbers, the mentally and spiritually poor. The hands of no one need lie idle a moment for lack of work, for it is no vague form of speech to say that the harvest is great and the laborers few.

There were ripe harvest-fields around Ivy Cliff, though Irene had not observed the golden grain bending its head for the sickle until Rose led her feet in the right direction. Not many of the naturally poor were around them, yet some required even bodily ministrations - children, the sick and the aged. The destitution that most prevailed was of the mind; and this is the saddest form of poverty. Mental hunger! how it exhausts the soul and debases its heaven-born faculties, sinking it into a gross corporeal sphere, that is only a little removed from the animal! To feed the hungry and clothe the naked mean a great deal more than the bestowal of food and raiment; yes, a great deal more; and we have done but a small part of Christian duty - have obeyed only in the letter - when we supply merely the bread that perishes.

Rose Carman had been wisely instructed, and she was an apt scholar. Now, from a learner she became a teacher, and in the suffering Irene found one ready to accept the higher truths that governed her life, and to act with her in giving them a real ultimation. So, in the two years which had woven their web of new experiences for the heart of Irene, she had been drawn almost imperceptibly by Rose into fields of labor where the work that left her hands was, she saw, good work, and must endure for ever. What peace it often brought to her striving spirit, when, but for the sustaining and protecting power of good deeds, she would have been swept out upon the waves of turbulent passion - tossed and beaten there until her exhausted heart sunk down amid the waters, and lay dead for a while at the bottom of her great sea of trouble!

It was better - oh, how much better! - when she laid her head at night on her lonely pillow, to have in memory the face of a poor sick woman, which had changed from suffering to peace as she talked to her of higher things than the body's needs, and bore her mind up into a region of tranquil thought, than to be left with no image to dwell upon but an image of her own shattered hopes. Yes, this was far better; and by the power of such memories the unhappy one had many peaceful seasons and nights of sweet repose.

All around Ivy Cliff, Irene and Rose were known as ministrant spirits to the poor and humble. The father of Rose was a man of wealth, and she had his entire sympathy and encouragement. Irene had no regular duties at home, Margaret being housekeeper and directress in all departments. So there was nothing to hinder the free course of her will as to the employment

T. S. Arthur

of time. With all her pride of independence, the ease with which Mrs. Talbot drew Irene in one direction, and now Miss Carman in another, showed how easily she might be influenced when off her guard. This is true in most cases of your very self-willed people, and the reason why so many of them get astray. Only conceal the hand that leads them, and you may often take them where you will. Ah, if Hartley Emerson had been wise enough, prudent enough and loving enough to have influenced aright the fine young spirit he was seeking to make one with his own, how different would the result have been!

In the region round about, our two young friends came in time to be known as the "Sisters of Charity." It was not said of them mockingly, nor in gay depreciation, nor in mean ill-nature, but in expression of a common sentiment, that recognized their high, self-imposed mission.

Thus it had been with Irene since her return to the old home at Ivy Cliff.

CHAPTER XXII.

STRUCK DOWN.

YES, Irene had looked for this - looked for it daily for now more than a year. Still it came upon her with a shock that sent a strange, wild shudder through all her being. A divorce! She was less prepared for it than she had ever been.

What was beyond? Ah! that touched a chord which gave a thrill of pain. What was beyond? A new alliance, of course. Legal disabilities removed, Hartley Emerson would take upon himself new marriage vows. Could she say, "Yea, and amen" to this? No, alas! no. There was a feeling of intense, irrepressible anguish away down in heart-regions that lay far beyond the lead-line of prior consciousness. What did it mean? She asked herself the question with a fainting spirit. Had she not known herself? Were old states of tenderness, which she had believed crushed out and dead along ago, hidden away in secret places of her heart, and kept there safe from harm?

No wonder she sat pale and still, crumpling nervously that fatal document which had startled her with a new revelation of herself. There was love in her heart still, and she knew it not. For a long time she sat like one in a dream.

"God help me!" she said at length, looking around her in a wild, bewildered manner. "What does all this mean?"

There came at this moment a gentle tap at her door. She knew whose soft hand had given the sound.

"Irene," exclaimed Rose Carman, as she took the hand of her friend and looked into her changed countenance, "what ails you?"

Irene turned her face partly away to get control of its expression.

"Sit down, Rose," she said, as soon as she could trust herself to speak.

They sat down together, Rose troubled and wondering. Irene then handed her friend the notice which she had received. Miss Carman read it, but made no remark for some time.

"It has disturbed you," she said at length, seeing that Irene continued silent.

"Yes, more than I could have believed," answered Irene. Her voice had lost its familiar tones.

"You have expected this?"

"Yes."

"I thought you were prepared for it."

"And I am," replied Irene, speaking with more firmness of manner. "Expectation grows so nervous, sometimes, that when the event comes it falls upon us with a painful shock. This is my case now. I would have felt it less severely if it had occurred six months ago."

"What will you do?" asked Rose.

"Do?"

"Yes."

"What can I do?"

"Resist the application, if you will."

"But I will not," answered Irene, firmly. "He signifies his wishes in the case, and those wishes must determine everything. I will remain passive."

"And let the divorce issue by default of answer?"

"Yes."

There was a faintness of tone which Rose could not help remarking.

"Yes," Irene added, "he desires this complete separation, and I can have nothing to say in opposition. I left him, and have remained ever since a stranger to his home and heart. We are nothing to each other, and yet are bound together by the strongest of bonds. Why should he not wish to be released from these bonds? And if he desires it, I have nothing to say. We are divorced in fact - why then retain the form?"

"There may be a question of the fact," said Rose.

"Yes; I understand you. We have discussed that point fully. Your view may be right, but I do not see it clearly. I will at least retain passive. The responsibility shall rest with him."

No life or color came back to the face of Irene. She looked as cold as marble; not cold without feeling, but with intense feeling recorded as in a piece of sculpture.

There were deeds of kindness and mercy set down in the purposes of our young friend, and it was to go forth and perform them that Rose had called for Irene this morning. But only one Sister of Charity went to the field that day, and only one for many days afterward.

Irene could not recover from the shock of this legal notice. It found her less prepared than she had been at any time during the last two years of separation. Her life at Ivy Cliff had not been favorable to a spirit of antagonism and accusation, nor favorable to a self-approving judgment of herself when the past came up, as it often came, strive as she would to cover it as with a veil. She had grown in this night of suffering, less self-willed and blindly impulsive. Some scales had dropped from her eyes, and she saw clearer. Yet no repentance for that one act of her life, which involved a series of consequences beyond the reach of conjecture, had found a place in her heart. There was no looking back from this - no sober questioning as to the right or necessity which had been involved. There had been one great mistake - so she decided the case - and that was the marriage.

From this fatal error all subsequent evil was born.

Months of waiting and expectation followed, and then

came a decree annulling the marriage.

"It is well," was the simple response of Irene when notice of the fact reached her.

Not even to Rose Carman did she reveal a thought that took shape in her mind, nor betray a single emotion that trembled in her heart. If there had been less appearance of indifference - less avoidance of the subject - her friends would have felt more comfortable as to her state of mind. The unnatural repose of, exterior was to them significant of a strife within which she wished to conceal from all eyes.

About this time her true, loving friend, Miss Carman, married. Irene did not stand as one of the bridesmaids at the ceremony. Rose gently hinted her wishes in the case, but Irene shrunk from the position, and her feeling was respected. The husband of Rose was a merchant, residing in New York, named Everet. After a short bridal tour she went to her new home in the city. Mr. Everet was five or six years her senior, and a man worthy to be her life-companion. No sudden attachment had grown up between them. For years they had been in the habit of meeting, and in this time the character of each had been clearly read by the other. When Mr. Everet asked the maiden's hand, it, was yielded without a sign of hesitation.

The removal of Rose from the neighborhood of Ivy Cliff greatly disturbed the even-going tenor of Irene's life. It withdrew also a prop on which she had leaned often in times of weakness, which would recur very heavily.

"How can I live without you?" she said in tears, as she

sat alone with the new-made bride on the eve of her departure; "you have been everything to me, Rose - strength in weakness; light, when all around was cold and dark; a guide when I had lost my way. God bless and make you happy, darling! And he will. Hearts like yours create happiness wherever they go."

"My new home will only be a few hours' distant," replied Rose; "I shall see you there often."

Irene sighed. She had been to the city only a few times since that sad day of separation from her husband. Could she return again and enter one of its bright social circles? Her heart said no. But love drew her too strongly. In less than a month after Rose became the mistress of a stately mansion, Irene was her guest. This was just six years from the time when she set up her home there, a proud and happy young wife. Alas! that hearth was desolate, "its bright fire quenched and gone."

It was best for Irene thus to get back again into a wider social sphere - to make some new friends, and those of a class that such a woman as Mrs. Everet would naturally draw around her. Three years of suffering, and the effort to lead a life of self-denial and active interest in others, had wrought in Irene a great change. The old, flashing ardor of manner was gone. If she grew animated in conversation, as she often did from temperament, her face would light up beautifully, but it did not show the radiance of old times. Thought, more than feeling, gave its living play to her countenance. All who met her were attracted; as her history was known, observation naturally took the form of close scrutiny. People wished to find the angular and repellant sides of her character in order to see how far she might be to blame. But they were not able to discover them. On the subjects of woman's rights, domestic tyranny, sexual equality and all kindred themes she was guarded in speech. She never introduced them herself, and said but little when they formed the staple of conversation.

Even if, in three years of intimate, almost daily, association with Rose, she had not learned to think in some new directions on these bewildering questions, certain womanly instincts must have set a seal upon her lips. Not for all the world would she, to a stranger - no, nor to any new friend - utter a sentiment that could in the least degree give color to the thought that she wished to throw even the faintest shadow of blame on Hartley Emerson. Not that she was ready to take blame to herself, or give the impression that fault rested by her door. No. The subject was sacred to herself, and she asked no sympathy and granted no confidences. There were those who sought to draw her out, who watched her face and words with keen intentness when certain themes were discussed. But they were unable to reach the penetralia of her heart. There was a chamber of record there into which no one could enter but herself.

Since the separation of Irene from her husband, Mr. Delancy had shown signs of rapid failure. His heart was bound up in his daughter, who, with all her captious self-will and impulsiveness, loved him with a tenderness and fervor that never knew change or eclipse. To see her make shipwreck of life's dearest hopes - to know that her name was spoken by hundreds in reprobation - to look daily on her quiet, changing, suffering face, was more than his fond heart could bear. It broke him down. This fact, more perhaps, than her own sad experiences, tended to sober the mind of Irene, and leave it almost passive under the right influences of her wise young friend.

After the removal of Rose from the neighborhood of Ivy Cliff, the health of Mr. Delancy failed still more rapidly, and in a few months the brief visits of Irene to her friend in New York had to be intermitted. She could no longer venture to leave her father, even under the care of their faithful Margaret. A sad winter for Irene succeeded. Mr. Delancy drooped about until after Christmas, in a weary, listless way, taking little interest in anything, and bearing both physical and mental consciousness as a burden it would be pleasant to lay down. Early in January he had to give up and go to bed; and now the truth of his condition startled the mind of Irene and filled her with alarm. By slow, insidious encroachments, that dangerous enemy, typhoid fever, had gained a lodgment in the very citadel of life, and boldly revealed itself, defying the healer's art. For weeks the dim light of mortal existence burned with a low, wavering flame, that any sudden breath of air might extinguish; then it grew steady again, increased, and sent a few brighter rays into the darkness which had gathered around Ivy Cliff.

Spring found Mr. Delancy strong enough to sit, propped up with pillows, by the window of his chamber, and look out upon the newly-mantled trees, the green fields, and the bright river flashing in the sunshine. The heart of Irene took courage again. The cloud which had lain upon it all winter like a funereal pall dissolved, and went floating away and wasting itself in dim expanses.

Alas, that all this sweet promise was but a mockery of

hope! A sudden cold, how taken it was almost impossible to tell - for Irene guarded her father as tenderly as if he were a new-born infant - disturbed life's delicate equipoise, and the scale turned fatally the wrong way.

Poor Irene! She had only staggered under former blows - this one struck her down. Had life anything to offer now? "Nothing! nothing!" she said in her heart, and prayed that she might die and be at rest with her father.

Months of stupor followed this great sorrow; then her heart began to beat again with some interest in life. There was one friend, almost her only friend - for she now repelled nearly every one who approached her - who never failed in hopeful, comforting, stimulating words and offices, who visited her frequently in her recluse life at Ivy Cliff, and sought with untiring assiduity to win her once more away from its dead seclusion. And she was at last successful. In the winter after Mr. Delancy's death, Irene, after much earnest persuasion, consented to pass a few weeks in the city with Mrs. Everet. This gained, her friend was certain of all the rest.

CHAPTER XXIII.

THE HAUNTED VISION.

GRADUALLY the mind of Irene attained clearness of perception as to duty, and a firmness of will that led her to act in obedience to what reason and religion taught her was right. The leading idea which Mrs. Everet endeavored to keep before her was this: that no happiness is possible, except in some work that removes self-consciousness and fills our minds with an interest in the well-being of others. While Rose was at Ivy Cliff, Irene acted with her, and was sustained by her love and companionship. After her marriage and removal to New York, Irene was left to stand alone, and this tried her strength. It was feeble. The sickness and death of her father drew her back again into herself, and for a time extinguished all interest in what was on the outside. To awaken a new and higher life was the aim of her friend, and she never wearied in her generous efforts. During this winter plans were matured for active usefulness in the old spheres, and Mrs. Everet promised to pass as much time in the next summer with her father as possible, so as to act with Irene in the development of these schemes.

The first warm days of summer found Irene back again in her home at Ivy Cliff. Her visit in New York had been prolonged far beyond the limit assigned to it in the beginning, but Rose would not consent to an earlier return. This winter of daily life with Mrs. Everet, in the unreserved intercourse of home, was of great use to Irene. Affliction had mellowed all the harder portions of her disposition, which the trouble and experiences of the past few years could not reach with their softening influences. There was good soil in her mind, well prepared, and the sower failed not in the work of scattering good seed upon it with a liberal hand - seed that felt soon a quickening life and swelled in the delight of coming germination.

It is not our purpose to record the history of Irene during the years of her discipline at Ivy Cliff, where she lived, nun-like, for the larger part of her time. She had useful work there, and in its faithful performance peace came to her troubled soul. Three or four times every year she paid a visit to Rose, and spent on each occasion from one to three or four weeks. It could not but happen that in these visits congenial friendship would be made, and tender remembrances go back with her into the seclusion of her country home, to remain as sweet companions in her hours of loneliness.

It was something remarkable that, during the six or seven years which followed Irene's separation from her husband, she had never seen him. He was still a resident of New York, and well known as a rapidly advancing member of the bar. Occasionally his name met her eyes in the newspapers, as connected with some important suit; but, beyond this, his life was to her a dead letter. He might be married again, for all she knew to the contrary. But she never dwelt on that thought; its intrusion always disturbed her, and that profoundly.

T. S. Arthur

And how was it with Hartley Emerson? Had he again tried the experiment which once so signally failed? No; he had not ventured upon the sea whose depths held the richest vessel he had freighted in life. Visions of loveliness had floated before him, and he had been lured by them, a few times, out of his beaten path. But he carried in his memory a picture that, when his eyes turned inward, held their gaze so fixedly that all other images grew dim or unlovely. And so, with a sigh, he would turn again to the old way and move on as before.

But the past was irrevocable. "And shall I," he began to say to himself, "for this one great error of my youth - this blind mistake - pass a desolate and fruitless life?"

Oftener and oftener the question was repeated in his thoughts, until it found answer in an emphatic No! Then he looked around with a new interest, and went more into society. Soon one fair face came more frequently before the eyes of his mind than any other face. He saw it as he sat in his law-office, saw it on the page of his book as he read in the evening, lying over the printed words and hiding from his thoughts their meaning; saw it in dreams. The face haunted him. How long was this since that fatal night of discord and separation? Ten years. So long? Yes, so long. Ten weary years had made their record upon his book of life and upon hers. Ten weary years! The discipline of this time had not worked on either any moral deterioration. Both were yet sound to the core, and both were building up characters based on the broad foundations of virtue.

Steadily that face grew into a more living distinctness, haunting his daily thoughts and nightly visions. Then new life-pulses began to throb in his heart; new emotions to tremble over its long calm surface; new warmth to flow, spring-like, into the indurated soil. This face, which had begun thus to dwell with him, was the face of a maiden, beautiful to look upon. He had met her often during a year, and from the beginning of their acquaintance she had interested him. If he erred not, the interest was mutual. prom all points of view he now commenced studying her character. Having made one mistake, he was fearful and guarded. Better go on a lonely man to the end of life than again have his love-freighted bark buried in mid-ocean.

At last, Emerson was satisfied. He had found the sweet being whose life could blend in eternal oneness with his own; and it only remained for him to say to her in words what she had read as plainly as written language in his eyes. So far as she was concerned, no impediment existed. We will not say that she was ripe enough in soul to wed with this man, who had passed through experiences of a kind that always develop the character broadly and deeply. No, for such was not the case. She was too young and inexperienced to understand him; too narrow in her range of thought; too much a child. But something in her beautiful, innocent, sweet young face had won his heart; and in the weakness of passion, not in the manly strength of a deep love, he had bowed down to a shrine at which he could never worship and be satisfied.

But even strong men are weak in woman's toils, and Hartley Emerson was a captive.

There was to be a pleasure-party on one of the steamers that cut the bright waters of the fair Hudson, and Emerson and the maiden, whose face was now his daily companion, were to be of the number. He felt that the time had come for him to speak if he meant to speak at all - to say what was in his thought, or turn aside and let another woo and win the lovely being imagination had already pictured as the sweet companion of his future home. The night that preceded this excursion was a sleepless one for Hartley Emerson. Questions and doubts, scarcely defined in his thoughts before, pressed themselves upon him and demanded a solution. The past came up with a vividness not experienced for years. In states of semi-consciousness - half-sleeping, half-waking - there returned to him such life-like realizations of events long ago recorded in his memory, and covered over with the dust of time, that he started from them to full wakefulness, with a heart throbbing in wild tumult. Once there was presented so vivid a picture of Irene that for some moments he was unable to satisfy himself that all these ten years of loneliness were not a dream. He saw her as she stood before him on that ever-to-be-remembered night and said, "*I go!*" Let us turn back and read the record of her appearance as he saw her then and now:

"She had raised her eyes from the floor, and turned them full upon her husband. Her face was not so pale. Warmth had come back to the delicate skin, flushing it with beauty. She did not stand before him an impersonation of anger, dislike or rebellion. There was not a repulsively attitude or expression. No flashing of the eyes, nor even the cold, diamond glitter seen a little while before. Slowly turning away, she left the room. But to her husband she seemed still standing there, a lovely vision. There had fallen, in that instant of time, a sunbeam, which fixed the image upon his memory in imperishable colors."

Emerson groaned as he fell back upon his pillow and shut his eyes. What would he not then have given for one full draught of Lethe's fabled waters.

Morning came at last, its bright beams dispersing the shadows of night; and with it came back the warmth of his new passion and his purpose on that day, if the opportunity came, to end all doubt, by offering the maiden his hand - we do not say heart, for of that he was not the full possessor.

The day opened charmingly, and the pleasure-party were on the wing betimes. Emerson felt a sense of exhilaration as the steamer passed out from her moorings and glided with easy grace along the city front. He stood upon her deck with a maiden's hand resting on his arm, the touch of which, though light as the pressure of a flower, was felt with strange distinctness. The shadows of the night, which had brooded so darkly over his spirit, were gone, and only a dim remembrance of the gloom remained. Onward the steamer glided, sweeping by the crowded line of buildings and moving grandly along, through palisades of rock on one side and picturesque landscapes on the other, until bolder scenery stretched away and mountain barriers raised themselves against the blue horizon.

There was a large number of passengers on board, scattered over the decks or lingering in the cabins, as inclination prompted. The observer of faces and character had field enough for study; but Hartley Emerson was not inclined to read in the book of character on this occasion. One subject occupied his thoughts to the exclusion of all others. There had come a period that was full of interest and fraught with momentous consequences which must extend through all of his after years. He saw little but the maiden at his side - thought of little but his purpose to ask her to walk with him, a soul-companion, in the journey of life.

During the first hour there was a constant moving to and fro and the taking up of new positions by the passengers - a hum and buzz of conversation - laughing - exclamations - gay talk and enthusiasm. Then a quieter tone prevailed. Solitary individuals took places of observation; groups seated themselves in pleasant circles to chat, and couples drew away into cabins or retired places, or continued the promenade.

Among the latter were Emerson and his companion. Purposely he had drawn the fair girl away from their party, in order to get the opportunity he desired. He did not mean to startle her with an abrupt proposal here, in the very eye of observation, but to advance toward the object by slow approaches, marking well the effect of his words, and receding the moment he saw that, in beginning to comprehend him, her mind showed repulsion or marked disturbance.

Thus it was with them when the boat entered the Highlands and swept onward with wind-like speed. They were in one of the gorgeously furnished cabins, sitting together on a sofa. There had been earnest talk, but on some subject of taste. Gradually Emerson changed the theme and began approaching the one nearest to his heart. Slight embarrassment followed; his voice took on a different tone; it was lower, tenderer, more deliberate and impressive. He leaned closer, and the maiden did not retire; she understood him, and was waiting the pleasure of his speech with heart-throbbings that seemed as if they must be audible in his ears as well as her own.

The time had come. Everything was propitious. The words that would have sealed his fate and hers were on his lips, when, looking up, he knew not why, but under an impulse of the moment, he met two calm eyes resting upon him with an expression that sent the blood leaping back to his heart. Two calm eyes and a pale, calm face were before him for a moment; then they vanished in the crowd. But he knew them, though ten years lay between the last vision and this.

The words that were on his lips died unspoken. He could not have uttered them if life or death hung on the issue. No - no - no. A dead silence followed.

"Are you ill?" asked his companion, looking at him anxiously.

"No, oh no," he replied, trying to rally himself.

"But you are ill, Mr. Emerson. How pale your face is!"

"It will pass off in a moment." He spoke with an effort to appear self-possessed. "Let us go on deck," he added, rising. "There are a great many people in the cabin, and the atmosphere is oppressive."

A dead weight fell upon the maiden's heart as she arose and went on deck by the side of Mr. Emerson. She had noticed his sudden pause and glance across the cabin at the instant she was holding her breath for his next words, but did not observe the object, a sight of which had wrought on him so remarkable a change. They walked nearly the entire length of the boat, after getting on deck, before Mr. Emerson spoke. He then remarked on the boldness of the scenery and pointed out interesting localities, but in so absent and preoccupied a way that his companion listened without replying. In a little while he managed to get into the neighborhood of three or four of their party, with whom he left her, and, moving away, took a position on the upper deck just over the gangway from which the landings were made. Here he remained until the boat came to at a pier on which his feet had stepped lightly many, many times. Ivy Cliff was only a little way distant, hidden from view by a belt of forest trees. The ponderous machinery stood still, the plunging wheels stopped their muffled roar, and in the brooding silence that followed three or four persons stepped on the plank which had been thrown out and passed to the shore. A single form alone fixed the eyes of Hartley Emerson. He would have known it on the instant among a thousand. It was that of Irene. Her step was slow, like one abstracted in mind or like one in feeble health. After gaining the landing, she stood still and turned toward the boat, when their eyes met again - met, and held each other, by a spell which neither had power to break. The fastenings were thrown off, the engineer rung his bell; there was a clatter of machinery, a rush of waters and the boat glanced onward. Then Irene started like one suddenly aroused from sleep and walked rapidly away.

And thus they met for the first time after a separation of ten years.

CHAPTER XXIV.

THE MINISTERING ANGEL.

A CLATTER of machinery, a rush of waters, and the boat glanced onward but still Hartley Emerson stood motionless and statue-like, his eyes fixed upon the shore, until the swiftly-gliding vessel bore him away, and the object which had held his vision by a kind of fascination was concealed from view.

"An angel, if there ever was one on this side of heaven!" said a voice close to his ear. Emerson gave a start and turned quickly. A man plainly dressed stood beside him. He was of middle age, and had a mild, grave, thoughtful countenance.

"Of whom do you speak?" asked Emerson, not able entirely to veil his surprise.

"Of the lady we saw go ashore at the landing just now. She turned and looked at us. You could not help noticing her."

"Who is she?" asked Emerson, and then held his breath awaiting the answer. The question was almost involuntary, yet prompted by a suddenly awakened desire to bear the world's testimony regard to Irene.

"You don't know her, then?" remarked the stranger.

"I asked who she was." Emerson intended to say this firmly, but his voice was unsteady. "Let us sit down," he added, looking around, and then leading the way to where some unoccupied chairs were standing. By the time they were seated he had gained the mastery over himself.

"You don't know her, then?" said the man, repeating his words. "She is well known about these parts, I can assure you. Why, that was old Mr. Delancy's daughter. Did you never hear of her?"

"What about her?" was asked.

"Well, in the first place, she was married some ten or twelve years ago to a lawyer down in New York; and, in the second place, they didn't live very happily together - why, I never heard. I don't believe it was her fault, for she's the sweetest, kindest, gentlest lady it has ever been my good fortune to meet. Some people around Ivy Cliff call her the 'Angel,' and the word has meaning in it as applied to her. She left her husband, and he got a divorce, but didn't charge anything wrong against her. That, I suppose, was more than he dared to do, for a snow-flake is not purer."

"You have lived in the neighborhood?" said Emerson, keeping his face a little averted.

"Oh yes, sir. I have lived about here pretty much all my life."

"Then you knew Miss Delancy before she was married?"

"No, sir; I can't say that I knew much about her before that time. I used to see her now and then as she rode about the neighborhood. She was a gay, wild girl, sir. But that unhappy marriage made a great change in her. I cannot forget the first time I saw her after she came back to her father's. She seemed to me older by many years than when I last saw her, and looked like one just recovered from a long and serious illness. The brightness had passed from her face, the fire from her eyes, the spring from her footsteps. I believe she left her husband of her own accord, but I never knew that she made any complaint against him. Of course, people were very curious to know why she had abandoned him. But her lips must have been sealed, for only a little vague talk went floating around. I never heard a breath of wrong charged against him as coming from her."

Emerson's face was turned still more away from his companion, his eyes bent down and his brows firmly knit. He did not ask farther, but the man was on a theme that interested him, and so continued.

"For most of the time since her return to Ivy Cliff the life of Miss Delancy has been given to Christian charities. The death of her father was a heavy stroke. It took the life out of her for a while. Since her recovery from that shock she has been constantly active among us in good deeds. Poor sick women know the touch of her gentle hand and the music of her voice. She has brought sunlight into many wintry homes, and kindled again on hearths long desolate the fires of loving kindness. There must have been some lack of true appreciation on the part of her husband, sir. Bitter fountains do not send forth sweet waters like these. Don't you think so?"

"How should I know?" replied Emerson, a little coldly. The question was sprung upon him so suddenly that his answer was given in confusion of thought.

"We all have our opinions, sir," said the man, "and this seems a plain case. I've heard said that her husband was a hot-headed, self-willed, ill-regulated young fellow, no more fit to get married than to be President. That he didn't understand the woman - or, maybe, I should say child - whom he took for his wife is very certain, or he never would have treated her in the way he did!"

"How did he treat her?" asked Mr. Emerson.

"As to that," replied his talkative companion, "we don't know anything certain. But we shall not go far wrong in guessing that it was neither wise nor considerate. In fact, he must have outraged her terribly."

"This, I presume, is the common impression about Ivy Cliff?"

"No," said the man; "I've heard him well spoken of. The fact is, people are puzzled about the matter. We can't just understand it. But, I'm all on her side."

"I wonder she has not married again?" said Emerson. "There are plenty of men who would be glad to wed so perfect a being as you represent her to be."

"She marry!" There was indignation and surprise in the man's voice.

"Yes; why not?"

"Sir, she is a Christian woman!"

"I can believe that, after hearing your testimony in regard to her," said Emerson. But he still kept his face so much turned aside that its expression could not be seen.

"And reads her Bible."

"As we all should."

"And, what is more, believes in it," said the man emphatically.

"Don't all Christian people believe in the Bible?" asked Mr. Emerson.

"I suppose so, after a fashion; and a very queer fashion it is, sometimes."

"How does this lady of whom you speak believe in it differently from some others?"

"In this, that it means what it says on the subject of divorce."

"Oh, I understand. You think that if she were to marry again it would be in the face of conscientious scruples?"

"I do."

Mr. Emerson was about asking another question when one of the party to which he belonged joined him, and so the strange interview closed. He bowed to the man with whom he had been conversing, and then passed to another part of the boat.

With slow steps, that were unsteady from sudden weakness, Irene moved along the road that led to her home. After reaching the grounds of Ivy Cliff she turned aside into a small summer-house, and sat down at one of the windows that looked out upon the river as it stretched upward in its gleaming way. The boat she bad just left was already far distant, but it fixed her eyes, and they saw no other object until it passed from view around a wooded point of land. And still she sat motionless, looking at the spot where it had vanished from her sight.

"Miss Irene!" exclaimed Margaret, the faithful old domestic, who still bore rule at the homestead, breaking in upon her reverie, "what in the world are you doing here? I expected you up to-day, and when the boat stopped at the landing and you didn't come, I was uneasy and couldn't rest. Why child, what is the matter? You're sick!"

"Oh no, Margaret, I'm well enough," said Irene, trying to smile indifferently. And she arose and left the summer-house.

Kind, observant old Margaret was far from being satisfied, however. She saw that Irene was not as when she departed for the city a week before. If she were not sick in body, she was troubled in her mind, for her countenance was so changed that she could not look upon it without feeling a pang in her heart.

"I'm sure you're sick, Miss Irene," she said as they entered the house. "Now, what is the matter? What can I do or get for you ? Let me send over for

Dr. Edmondson?"

"No, no, my good Margaret, don't think of such a thing," replied Irene. "I'm not sick."

"Something's the matter with you, child," persisted Margaret.

"Nothing that won't cure itself," said Irene, trying to speak cheerfully. "I'll go up to my room for a little while."

And she turned away from her kind-hearted domestic. On entering her chamber Irene locked the door in order to be safe from intrusion, for she knew that Margaret would not let half an hour pass without coming up to ask how she was. Sitting down by the window, she looked out upon the river, along whose smooth surface had passed the vessel in which, a little while before, she met the man once called by the name of husband - met him and looked into his face for the first time in ten long years! The meeting had disturbed her profoundly. In the cabin of that vessel she had seen him by the side of a fair young girl in earnest conversation; and she had watched with a strange, fluttering interest the play of his features. What was he saying to that fair young girl that she listened with such a breathless, waiting air? Suddenly he turned toward her, their eyes met and were spell-bound for moments. What did she read in his eyes in those brief moments? What did he read in hers? Both questions pressed themselves upon her thoughts as she retreated among the crowd of passengers, and then hid herself from the chance of another meeting until the boat reached the landing at Ivy Cliff. Why did she pause on the shore, and turn to look upon the crowded decks? She knew not. The act was involuntary. Again their eyes met - met and held each other until the receding vessel placed dim distance between them.

In less than half an hour Margaret's hand was on the door, but she could not enter. Irene had not moved from her place at the window in all that time.

"Is that you, Margaret?" she called, starting from her abstraction.

"Do you want anything, Miss Irene?"

"No, thank you, Margaret."

She answered in as cheerful a tone as she could assume, and the kind old waiting-woman retired.

From that time every one noted a change in Irene. But none knew, or even guessed, its cause or meaning. Not even to her friend, Mrs. Everet, did she speak of her meeting with Hartley Emerson. Her face did not light up as before, and her eyes seemed always as if looking inward or gazing dreamily upon something afar off. Yet in good deeds she failed not. If her own heart was heavier, she made other hearts lighter by her presence.

And still the years went on in their steady revolutions - one, two, three, four, five more years, and in all that time the parted ones did not meet again.

CHAPTER XXV.

BORN FOR EACH OTHER.

I SAW Mr. Emerson yesterday," said Mrs. Everet. She was sitting with Irene in her own house in New York.

"Did you?" Irene spoke evenly and quietly, but did not turn her face toward Mrs. Everet.

"Yes. I saw him at my husband's store. Mr. Everet has engaged him to conduct an important suit, in which many thousands of dollars are at stake."

"How does be look?" inquired Irene, without showing any feelings but still keeping her face turned from Mrs Everet.

"Well, I should say, though rather too much frosted for a man of his years."

"Gray, do you mean?" Irene manifested some surprise.

"Yes; his hair and beard are quite sprinkled with time's white snow-flakes."

"He is only forty," remarked Irene.

"I should say fifty, judging from his appearance."

"Only forty." And a faint sigh breathed on the lips of Irene. She did not look around at her friend but sat very still, with her face turned partly away. Mrs. Everet looked at her closely, to read, if possible, what was passing in her mind. But the countenance of Irene was too much hidden. Her attitude, however, indicated intentness of thought, though not disturbing thought.

"Rose," she said at length, "I grow less at peace with myself as the years move onward."

"You speak from some passing state of mind," suggested Mrs. Everet.

"No; from a gradually forming permanent state. Ten years ago I looked back upon the past in a stern, self-sustaining, martyr-spirit. Five years ago all things wore a different aspect. I began to have misgivings; I could not so clearly make out my case. New thoughts on the subject - and not very welcome ones - began to intrude. I was self-convicted of wrong; yes, Rose, of a great and an irreparable wrong. I shut my eyes; I tried to look in other directions; but the truth, once seen, could not pass from the range of mental vision. I have never told you that I saw Mr. Emerson five years ago. The effect of that meeting was such that I could not speak of it, even to you. We met on one of the river steamboats - met and looked into each other's eyes for just a moment. It may only be a fancy of mine, but I have thought sometimes that, but for this seemingly accidental meeting, he would have married again."

"Why do you think so?" asked Mrs. Everet.

Irene did not answer for some moments. She hardly dared venture to put what she had seen in words. It was something that she felt more like hiding even from her own consciousness, if that were possible. But, having ventured so far, she could not well hold back. So she replied, keeping her voice into as dead a level as it was possible to assume:

"He was sitting in earnest conversation with a young lady, and from the expression of her face, which I could see, the subject on which he was speaking was evidently one in which more than her thought was interested. I felt at the time that he was on the verge of a new life-experiment - was about venturing upon a sea on which he had once made shipwreck. Suddenly he turned half around and looked at me before I had time to withdraw my eyes - looked at me with a strange, surprised, startled look. In another moment a form came between us; when it passed I was lost from his gaze in the crowd of passengers. I have puzzled myself a great many times over that fact of his turning his eyes, as if from some hidden impulse, just to the spot where I was sitting. There are no accidents - as I have often heard you say - in the common acceptation of the term; therefore this was no accident."

"It was a providence," said Rose.

"And to what end?" asked Irene.

Mrs. Everet shook her head.

"I will not even presume to conjecture."

Irene sighed, and then sat lost in thought. Recovering herself, she said:

" Since that time I have been growing less and less

satisfied with that brief, troubled portion of my life which closed so disastrously. I forgot how much the happiness of another was involved. A blind, willful girl, struggling in imaginary bonds, I thought only of myself, and madly rent apart the ties which death only should have sundered. For five years, Rose, I have carried in my heart the expression which looked out upon me from the eyes of Mr. Emerson at that brief meeting. Its meaning was not then, nor is it now, clear. I have never set myself to the work of interpretation, and believe the task would be fruitless. But whenever it is recalled I am affected with a tender sadness. And so his head is already frosted, Rose?"

"Yes."

"Though in years he has reached only manhood's ripened state. How I have marred his life! Better, far better, would it have been for him if I had been the bride of Death on my wedding-day!"

A shadow of pain darkened her face.

"No," replied Mrs. Everet; "it is better for both you and him that you were not the bride of Death. There are deeper things hidden in the events of life than our reason can fathom. We die when it is best for ourselves and best for others that we should die - never before. And the fact that we live is in itself conclusive that we are yet needed in the world by all who can be affected by our mortal existence."

"Gray hairs at forty!" This seemed to haunt the mind of Irene.

" It may be constitutional , " suggested Mrs. Everet;

"some heads begin to whiten at thirty."

"Possibly."

But the tone expressed no conviction.

"How was his face?" asked Irene.

"Grave and thoughtful. At least so it appeared to me."

"At forty." It was all Irene said.

Mrs. Everet might have suggested that a man of his legal position would naturally be grave and thoughtful, but she did not.

"It struck me," said Mrs. Everet, "as a true, pure, manly face. It was intellectual and refined; delicate, yet firm about the mouth and expansive in the upper portions. The hair curled softly away from his white temples and forehead."

"Worthy of a better fate!" sighed Irene. "And it is I who have marred his whole life! How blind is selfish passion! Ah, my friend, the years do not bring peace to my soul. There have been times when to know that he had sought refuge from a lonely life in marriage would have been a relief to me. Were this the case, the thought of his isolation, of his imperfect life, would not be for ever rebuking me. But now, while no less severely rebuked by this thought, I feel glad that he has not ventured upon an act no clear sanction for which is found in the Divine law. He could not, I feel, have remained so true and pure a man as I trust he is this day. God help him to hold on, faithful to his highest intuitions, even unto the end."

Mrs. Everet looked at Irene wonderingly as she spoke. She had never before thus unveiled her thoughts.

"He struck me," was her reply, "as a man who had passed through years of discipline and gained the mastery of himself."

"I trust that it may be so," Irene answered, rather as if speaking to herself than to another.

"As I grow older," she added, after a long pause, now looking with calm eyes upon her friend, "and life-experiences correct my judgment and chasten my feelings, I see all things in a new aspect. I understand my own heart better - its needs, capacities and yearnings; and self-knowledge is the key by which we unlock the mystery of other souls. So a deeper self-acquaintance enables me to look deeper into the hearts of all around me. I erred in marrying Mr. Emerson. We were both too hasty, self-willed and tenacious of rights and opinions to come together in a union so sacred and so intimate. But, after I had become his wife, after I had taken upon myself such holy vows, it was my duty to stand fast. I could not abandon my place and be innocent before God and man. And I am not innocent, Rose."

The face of Irene was strongly agitated for some moments; but she recovered herself and went on:

"I am speaking of things that have hitherto been secrets of my own heart. I could not bring them out even for you to look at, my dearest, truest, best of friends. Now it seems as if I could not bear the weight of my heavy thoughts alone; as if, in admitting you beyond the veil, I might find strength to suffer, if not ease from pain.

There is no such thing as living our lives over again and correcting their great errors. The past is an irrevocable fact. Ah, if conscience would sleep, if struggles for a better life would make atonement for wrong - then, as our years progress, we might lapse into tranquil states. But gradually clearing vision increases the magnitude of a fault like mine, for its fatal consequences are seen in broader light. There is a thought which has haunted me for a year past like a spectre. It comes to me unbidden; sometimes to disturb the quiet of my lonely evenings, sometimes in the silent night-watches to banish sleep from my pillow; sometimes to place silence on my lips as I sit among cherished friends. I never imagined that I would put this thought in words for any mortal ear; yet it is coming to my lips now, and I feel impelled to go on. You believe that there are, as you call them 'conjugal partners,' or men and women born for each other, who, in a true marriage of souls, shall become eternally one. They do not always meet in this life; nay, for the sake of that discipline which leads to purification, may form other and uncongenial ties in the world, and live unhappily; but in heaven they will draw together by a divinely-implanted attraction, and be there united for ever. I have felt that something like this must be true; that every soul must have its counterpart. The thought which has so haunted me is, that Hartley Emerson and unhappy *I* were born for each other."

She paused and looked with a half-startled air upon Mrs. Everet to mark the effect of this revelation. But Rose made no response and showed no surprise, however she might have been affected by the singular admission of her friend.

"It has been all in vain," continued Irene "that I have

pushed the thought aside - called it absurd, insane, impossible - back it would come and take its old place. And, stranger still, out of facts that I educed to prove its fallacy would come corroborative suggestions. I think it is well for my peace of mind that I have not been in the way of hearing about him or of seeing him. Since we parted it has been as if a dark curtain had fallen between us; and, so far as I am concerned, that curtain has been lifted up but once or twice, and then only for a moment of time. So all my thoughts of him are joined to the past. Away back in that sweet time when the heart of girlhood first thrills with the passion of love are some memories that haunt my soul like dreams from Elysium. He was, in my eyes, the impersonation of all that was lovely and excellent; his presence made my sense of happiness complete; his voice touched my ears as the blending of all rich harmonies. But there fell upon him a shadow; there came hard discords in the music which had entranced my soul; the fine gold was dimmed. Then came that period of mad strife, of blind antagonism, in which we hurt each other by rough contact. Finally, we were driven far asunder, and, instead of revolving together around a common centre, each has moved in a separate orbit. For years that dark period of pain has held the former period of brightness in eclipse; but of late gleams from that better time have made their way down to the present. Gradually the shadows are giving away. The first state is coming to be felt more and more as the true state - as that in best agreement with what we are in relation to each other. It was the evil in us that met in such fatal antagonism - not the good; it was something that we must put off if we would rise from natural and selfish life into spiritual and heavenly life. It was our selfishness and passion that drove us asunder. Thus it is, dear Rose, that my thoughts have been wandering about in the maze of life that entangles me. In my isolation I have time enough for mental inversion - for self-exploration - for idle fancies, if you will. And so I have lifted the veil for you; uncovered my inner life; taken you into the sanctuary over whose threshold no foot but my own had ever passed."

There was too much in all this for Mrs. Everet to venture upon any reply that involved suggestion or advice. It was from a desire to look deeper into the heart of her friend that she had spoken of her meeting with Mr. Emerson. The glance she obtained revealed far more than her imagination had ever reached.

CHAPTER XXVI.

LOVE NEVER DIES.

THE brief meeting with Mrs. Everet had stirred the memory of old times in the heart of Mr. Emerson. With a vividness unknown for years, Ivy Cliff and the sweetness of many life-passages there came back to him, and set heart-pulses that he had deemed stilled for ever beating in tumultuous waves. When the business of the day was over he sat down in the silence of his chamber and turned his eyes inward. He pushed aside intervening year after year, until the long-ago past was, to his consciousness, almost as real as the living present. What he saw moved him deeply. He grew restless, then showed disturbance of manner. There was an effort to turn away from the haunting fascination of this long-buried, but now exhumed period; but the dust and scoria were removed, and it lifted, like another Pompeii, its desolate walls and silent chambers in the clear noon-rays of the present.

After a long but fruitless effort to bury the past again, to let the years close over it as the waves close over a treasure-laden ship, Mr. Emerson gave himself up to its thronging memories and let them bear him whither they would.

In this state of mind he unlocked one of the drawers in

a secretary and took therefrom a small box or casket. Placing this on a table, he sat down and looked at it for some minutes, as if in doubt whether it were best for him to go further in this direction. Whether satisfied or not, he presently laid his fingers upon the lid of the casket and slowly opened it. It contained only a morocco case. He touched this as if it were something precious and sacred. For some moments after it was removed he sat holding it in his hand and looking at the dark, blank surface, as a long-expected letter is sometimes held before the seal is broken and the contents devoured with impatient eagerness. At last his finger pressed the spring on which it had been resting, and he looked upon a young, sweet face, whose eyes gazed back into his with a living tenderness. In a little while his hand so trembled, and his eyes grew so dim, that the face was veiled from his sight. Closing the miniature, but still retaining it in his hand, he leaned back in his chair and remained motionless, with shut eyes, for a long time; then he looked at the fair young face again, conning over every feature and expression, until sad memories came in and veiled it again with tears.

"Folly! weakness!" he said at last, pushing the picture from him and making a feeble effort to get back his manly self-possession. "The past is gone for ever. The page on which its sad history is written was closed long ago, and the book is sealed. Why unclasp the volume and search for that dark record again?"

Yet, even as he said this, his hand reached out for the miniature, and his eyes were on it ere the closing words had parted from his lips.

" Poor Irene ! " he murmured , as he gazed on her

pictured face. "You had a pure, tender, loving heart -" then, suddenly shutting the miniature, with a sharp click of the spring, he tossed it from him upon the table and said,

"This is folly! folly! folly!" and, leaning back in his chair, he shut his eyes and sat for a long time with his brows sternly knitted together and his lips tightly compressed. Rising, at length, he restored the miniature to its casket, and the casket to its place in the drawer. A servant came to the door at this moment, bringing the compliments of a lady friend, who asked him, if not engaged, to favor her with his company on that evening, as she had a visitor, just arrived, to whom she wished to introduce him. He liked the lady, who was the wife of a legal friend, very well; but he was not always so well pleased with her lady friends, of whom she had a large circle. The fact was, she considered him too fine a man to go through life companionless, and did not hesitate to use every art in her power to draw him into an entangling alliance. He saw this, and was often more amused than annoyed by her finesse.

It was on his lips to send word that he was engaged, but a regard for truth would not let him make this excuse; so, after a little hesitation and debate, he answered that he would present himself during the evening. The lady's visitor was a widow of about thirty years of age - rich, educated, accomplished and personally attractive. She was from Boston, and connected with one of the most distinguished families in Massachusetts, whose line of ancestry ran back among the nobles of England. In conversation this lady showed herself to be rarely gifted, and there was a charm about her manners that was irresistible. Mr.

Emerson, who had been steadily during the past five years growing less and less attracted by the fine women he met in society, found himself unusually interested in Mrs. Eager.

"I knew you would like her," said his lady friend, as Mr. Emerson was about retiring at eleven o'clock.

"You take your conclusion for granted," he answered, smiling. "Did I say that I liked her?"

"We ladies have eyes," was the laughing rejoinder. "Of course you like her. She's going to spend three or four days with me. You'll drop in to-morrow evening. Now don't pretend that you have an engagement. Come; I want you to know her better. I think her charming."

Mr. Emerson did not promise positively, but said that he might look in during the evening.

For a new acquaintance, Mrs. Eager had attracted him strongly; and his thoughtful friend was not disappointed in her expectation of seeing him at her house on the succeeding night. Mrs. Eager, to whom the lady she was visiting had spoken of Mr. Emerson in terms of almost extravagant eulogy, was exceedingly well pleased with him, and much gratified at meeting him again, A second interview gave both an opportunity for closer observation, and when they parted it was with pleasant thoughts of each other lingering in their minds. During the time that Mrs. Eager remained in New York, which was prolonged for a week beyond the period originally fixed, Mr. Emerson saw her almost every day, and became her voluntary escort in visiting points of local interest. The more he saw of her the more he was charmed with her character. She seemed in his eyes the most attractive woman he had ever met. Still, there was something about her that did not wholly satisfy him, though what it was did not come into perception.

Five years had passed since any serious thought of marriage had troubled the mind of Mr. Emerson. After his meeting with Irene he had felt that another union in this world was not for him - that he had no right to exchange vows of eternal fidelity with any other woman. She had remained unwedded, and would so remain, he felt, to the end of her life. The legal contract between them was dissolved; but, since his brief talk with the stranger on the boat, he had not felt so clear as to the higher law obligations which were upon them. And so he had settled it in his mind to bear life's burdens alone.

But Mrs. Eager had crossed his way, and filled, in many respects, his ideal of a woman. There was a charm about her that won him against all resistance.

"Don't let this opportunity pass," said his interested lady friend, as the day of Mrs. Eager's departure drew nigh. "She is a woman in a thousand, and will make one of the best of wives. Think, too, of her social position, her wealth and her large cultivation. An opportunity like this is never presented more than once in a lifetime."

"You speak," replied Mr. Emerson, "as if I had only to say the word and this fair prize would drop into my arms."

"She will have to be wooed if she is won. Were this not the case she would not be worth having," said the lady. "But my word for it, if you turn wooer the winning will not be hard. If I have not erred in my observation, you are about mutually interested. There now, my cautious sir, if you do not get handsomely provided for, it will be no fault of mine."

In two days from this time Mrs. Eager was to return to Boston.

"You must take her to see those new paintings at the rooms of the Society Library to-morrow. I heard her express a desire to examine them before returning to Boston. Connoisseurs are in ecstasies over three or four of the pictures, and, as Mrs. Eager is something of an enthusiast in matters of art, your favor in this will give her no light pleasure."

"I shall be most happy to attend her," replied Mr. Emerson. "Give her my compliments, and say that, if agreeable to herself, I will call for her at twelve to-morrow."

"No verbal compliments and messages," replied the lady; "that isn't just the way."

"How then? Must I call upon her and deliver my message? That might not be convenient to me nor agreeable to her."

"Oh!" ejaculated the lady, with affected impatience, "you men are so stupid at times! You know how to write?"

"Ah! yes, I comprehend you now."

" Very well. Send your compliments and your message

in a note; and let it be daintily worded; not in heavy phrases, like a legal document."

"A very princess in feminine diplomacy!" said Mr. Emerson to himself, as he turned from the lady and took his way homeward. "So I must pen a note."

Now this proved a more difficult matter than he had at first thought. He sat down to the task immediately on returning to his room. On a small sheet of tinted note-paper he wrote a few words, but they did not please him, and the page was thrown into the fire. He tried again, but with no better success - again and again; but still, as he looked at the brief sentences, they seemed to express too much or too little. Unable to pen the note to his satisfaction, he pushed, at last, his writing materials aside, saying,

"My head will be clearer and cooler in the morning."

It was drawing on to midnight, and Mr. Emerson had not yet retired. His thoughts were too busy for sleep. Many things were crowding into his mind - questions, doubts, misgivings - scenes from the past and imaginations of the future. And amid them all came in now and then, just for a moment, as he had seen it five years before, the pale, still face of Irene.

Wearied in the conflict, tired nature at last gave way, and Mr. Emerson fell asleep in his chair.

Two hours of deep slumber tranquilized his spirit. He awoke from this, put off his clothing and laid his head on his pillow. It was late in the morning when he arose. He had no difficulty now in penning a note to Mrs. Eager. It was the work of a moment, and satisfactory to him in the first effort.

At twelve he called with a carriage for the lady, whom he found all ready to accompany him, and in the best possible state of mind. Her smile, as he presented himself, was absolutely fascinating; and her voice seemed like a freshly-tuned instrument, every tone was so rich in musical vibration, and all the tones came chorded to his ear.

There were not many visitors at the exhibition rooms - a score, perhaps - but they were art-lovers, gazing in rapt attention or talking in hushed whispers. They moved about noiselessly here and there, seeming scarcely conscious that others were present. Gradually the number increased, until within an hour after they entered it was more than doubled. Still, the presence of art subdued all into silence or subdued utterances.

Emerson was charmed with his companion's appreciative admiration of many pictures. She was familiar with art-terms and special points of interest, and pointed out beauties and harmonies that to him were dead letters without an interpreter. They came, at last, to a small but wonderfully effective picture, which contained a single figure, that of a man sitting by a table in a room which presented the appearance of a library. He held a letter in his hand - a old letter; the artist had made this plain - but was not reading. He had been reading; but the words, proving conjurors, had summoned the dead past before him, and he was now looking far away, with sad, dreamy eyes, into the long ago. A casket stood open. Time letter had evidently been taken from this repository. There was a miniature; a bracelet of auburn hair; a ring and a chain of gold lying on the table. Mr. Emerson turned to the catalogue

T. S. Arthur

and read,

"WITH THE BURIED PAST."

And below this title the brief sentiment -

"Love never dies."

A deep, involuntary sigh came through his lips and stirred the pulseless air around him. Then, like an echo, there came to his ears an answering sigh, and, turning, he looked into the face of Irene! She had entered the rooms a little while before, and in passing from picture to picture had reached this one a few moments after Mr. Emerson. She had not observed him, and was just beginning to feel its meaning, when the sigh that attested its power over him reached her ears and awakened an answering sigh. For several moments their eyes were fixed in a gaze which neither had power to withdraw. The face of Irene had grown thinner, paler and more shadowy - if we may use that term to express something not of the earth, earthy - than it was when he looked upon it five years before. But her eyes were darker in contrast with her colorless face, and had a deeper tone of feeling.

They did not speak nor pass a sign of recognition. But the instant their eyes withdrew from each other Irene turned from the picture and left the rooms.

When Mr. Emerson looked back into the face of his companion, its charm was gone. Beside that of the fading countenance, so still and nun-like, upon which he had gazed a moment before, it looked coarse and worldly. When she spoke, her tones no longer came in chords of music to his ears, but jarred upon his feelings. He grew silent; cold, abstracted. The lady noted the change, and tried to rally him; but her efforts were vain. He moved by her side like an automaton, and listened to her comments on the pictures they paused to examine in such evident absent-mindedness that she became annoyed, and proposed returning home. Mr. Emerson made no objection, and they left the quiet picture-gallery for the turbulence of Broadway. The ride home was a silent one, and they separated in mutual embarrassment, Mr. Emerson going back to his rooms instead of to his office, and sitting down in loneliness there, with a shuddering sense of thankfulness at his heart for the danger he had just escaped.

"What a blind spell was on me!" he said, as he gazed away down into his soul - far, far deeper than any tone or look from Mrs. Eager had penetrated - and saw needs, states and yearnings there which must be filled or there could be no completeness of life. And now the still, pale face of Irene stood out distinctly; and her deep, weird, yearning eyes looked into his with a fixed intentness that stirred his heart to its profoundest depths.

Mr. Emerson was absent from his office all that day. But on the next morning he was at his post, and it would have taken a close observer to have detected any change in his usually quiet face. But there was a change in the man - a great change. He had gone down deeper into his heart than he had ever gone before, and understood himself better. There was little danger of his ever being tempted again in this direction.

CHAPTER XXVII.

EFFECTS OF THE STORM.

IT was more than a week before Mr. Emerson called again upon the lady friend who had shown so strong a desire to procure him a wife. He expected her to introduce the name of Mrs. Eager, and came prepared to talk in a way that would for ever close the subject of marriage between them. The lady expressed surprise at not having seen him for so long a time, and then introduced the subject nearest her thought.

"What was the matter with you and Mrs. Eager?" she asked, her face growing serious.

Mr. Emerson shook his head, and said, "Nothing," with not a shadow of concern in his voice.

"Nothing? Think again. I could hardly have been deceived."

"Why do you ask? Did the lady charge anything ungallant against me?"

Mr. Emerson was unmoved.

"Oh no, no! She scarcely mentioned your name after her return from viewing the pictures. But she was not in so bright a humor as when she went out, and was dull up to the hour of her departure for Boston. I'm afraid you offended her in some way - unconsciously on your part, of course."

"No, I think not," said Mr. Emerson. "She would be sensitive in the extreme if offended by any word or act of mine."

"Well, letting that all pass, Mr. Emerson, what do you think of Mrs. Eager?"

"That she is an attractive and highly accomplished woman."

"And the one who reaches your ideal of a wife?"

"No, ma'am," was the unhesitating answer, and made in so emphatic a tone that there was no mistaking his sincerity. There was a change in his countenance and manner. He looked unusually serious.

The lady tried to rally him, but he had come in too sober a state of mind for pleasant trifling on this subject, of all others.

"My kind, good friend," he said, "I owe you many thanks for the interest you have taken in me, and for your efforts to get me a companion. But I do not intend to marry."

"So you have said - "

"Pardon me for interrupting you." Mr. Emerson checked the light speech that was on her tongue. "I am going to say to you some things that have never passed my lips before. You will understand me; this I know, or I would not let a sentence come into utterance. And I know more, that you will not make light of what to me is sacred."

The lady was sobered in a moment.

"To make light of what to you is sacred would be impossible," she replied.

"I believe it, and therefore I am going to speak of things that are to me the saddest of my life, and yet are coming to involve the holiest sentiments. I have more than one reason for desiring now to let another look below the quiet surface; and I will lift the veil for your eyes alone. You know that I was married nearly twenty years ago, and that my wife separated herself from me in less than three years after our union; and you also know that the separation was made permanent by a divorce. This is all that you or any other one knows, so far as I have made communication on the subject; and I have reason to believe that she who was my wife has been as reserved in the matter as myself.

"The simple facts in the case are these: We were both young and undisciplined, both quick-tempered, self-willed, and very much inclined to have things our own way. She was an only child, and so was I. Each had been spoiled by long self-indulgence. So, when we came together in marriage, the action of our lives, instead of taking a common pulsation, was inharmonious. For a few years we strove together blindly in our bonds, and then broke madly asunder. I think we were about equally in fault; but if there was a preponderance of blame, it rested on my side, for, as a man, I should have kept a cooler head and shown greater forbearance. But the time for blame has long since passed. It is with the stern, irrevocable facts that we are dealing now.

"So bitter had been our experience, and so painful the shock of separation, that I think a great many years must have passed before repentance came into either heart - before a feeling of regret that we had not held fast to our marriage vows was born. How it was with me you may infer from the fact that, after the lapse of two years, I deliberately asked for and obtained a divorce on the ground of desertion. But doubt as to the propriety of this step stirred uneasily in my mind for the first time when I held the decree in my hand; and I have never felt wholly satisfied with myself since. There should be something deeper than incompatibility of temper to warrant a divorce. The parties should correct what is wrong in themselves, and thus come into harmony. There is no excuse for pride, passion and self-will. The law of God does not make these justifiable causes of divorce, and neither should the law of man. A purer woman than my wife never lived; and she had elements of character that promised a rare development. I was proud of her. Ah, if I had been wiser and more patient! If I had endeavored to lead, instead of assuming the manly prerogative! But I was young, and blind, and willful!

"Fifteen years have passed since the day we parted, and each has remained single. If we had not separated, we might now be living in a true heart-union; for I believe, strange as it may sound to you, that we were made for each other - that, when the false and evil of our lives are put off, the elements of conjunction will appear. We have made for ourselves of this world a dreary waste, when, if we had overcome the evil of our

　　　　　T. S. Arthur

hearts, our paths would have been through green and fragrant places. It may be happier for us in the next; and it will be. I am a better man, I think, for the discipline through which I have passed, and she is a better woman."

Mr. Emerson paused.

"She? Have you seen her?" the lady asked.

"Twice since we parted, and then only for a moment. Suddenly each time we met, and looked into each other's eyes for a single instant; then, as if a curtain had dropped suddenly between us, we were separated. But the impression of her face remained as vivid and permanent as a sun-picture. She lives, for most of her time, secluded at Ivy Cliff, her home on the Hudson; and her life is passed there, I hear, in doing good. And, if good deeds, from right ends, write their history on the human face, then her countenance bears the record of tenderest charities. It was pale when I last saw it - pale, but spiritual - I can use no other word; and I felt a sudden panic at the thought that she was growing into a life so pure and heavenly that I must stand afar off as unworthy. It had sometimes come into my thought that we were approaching each other, as both put off, more and more, the evil which had driven us apart and held us so long asunder. But this illusion our last brief meeting dispelled. She has passed me on the road of self-discipline and self-abnegation, and is journeying far ahead. And now I can but follow through life at a distance.

"So much, and no more, my friend. I drop the veil over my heart. You will understand me better hereafter. I shall not marry. That legal divorce is invalid. I could not perjure my soul by vows of fidelity toward another. Patiently and earnestly will I do my allotted work here. My better hopes lie all in the heavenly future.

"And now, my friend, we will understand each other better. You have looked deeper into my thoughts and experiences than any other human being. Let the revelation be sacred to yourself. The knowledge you possess may enable you to do me justice sometimes, and sometimes to save me from an intrusion of themes that cannot but touch me unpleasantly. There was a charm about Mrs. Eager that, striking me suddenly, for a little while bewildered my fancy. She is a woman of rare endowments, and I do not regret the introduction and passing influence she exercised over me. It was a dream from which the awakening was certain. Suddenly the illusion vanished, as I saw her beside my lost Irene. The one was of the earth, earthy - the other of heaven, heavenly; and as I looked back into her brilliant face, radiant with thought and feeling, I felt a low, creeping shudder, as if just freed from the spell of a siren. I cannot be enthralled again, even for a moment."

Back again into his world's work Mr. Emerson returned after this brief, exciting episode, and found in its performance from high and honorable motives that calmly sustaining power which comes only as the reward of duties faithfully done.

CHAPTER XXVIII.

AFTER THE STORM.

AFTER the storm! How long the treasure remained buried in deep waters! How long the earth showed unsightly furrows and barren places! For nearly twenty years there had been warm sunshine, and no failure of the dews nor the early and latter rain. But grass had not grown nor flowers blossomed in the path of that desolating tempest. Nearly twenty years! If the history of these two lives during that long period could be faithfully written, it would flood the soul with tears.

Four years later than the time when we last presented Irene to the reader we introduce her again. That meeting in the picture-gallery had disturbed profoundly the quiet pulses of her life. She did not observe Mr. Emerson's companion. The picture alone had attracted her attention; and she had just began to feel its meaning when an audible sigh reached her ears. The answering sigh was involuntary. Then they looked into each other's faces again - only for an instant - but with what a volume of mutual revelations!

It was four years subsequent to this time that Irene, after a brief visit in New York to her friend, Mrs. Everet, returned to her rural home. Mrs. Everet was to follow on the next day, and spend a few weeks with her father. It was yet in the early summer, and there were not many passengers on the-boat. As was usual, Irene provided herself with a volume, and soon after going on board took a retired place in one of the cabins and buried herself in its pages. For over three hours she remained completely absorbed in what she was reading. Then her mind began to wander and dwell on themes that made the even pulses of her heart beat to a quicker measure; yet still her eyes remained fixed on the book she held in her hand. At length she became aware that some one was near her, by the falling of a shadow on the page she was trying to read. Lifting her head, she met the eyes of Hartley Emerson. He was standing close to her, his hand resting on the back of a chair, which he now drew nearly in front of her.

"Irene," he said, in a low, quiet voice, "I am glad to meet you again in this world." And he reached out his hand as he spoke.

For a moment Irene sat very still, but she did not take her eyes from Mr. Emerson's face; then she extended her hand and let it lie in his. He did not fail to notice that it had a low tremor.

Thus received, he sat down.

"Nearly twenty years have passed, Irene, since a word or sign has passed between us."

Her lips moved, but there was no utterance.

"Why should we not, at least, be friends?"

Her lips moved again, but no words trembled on the air.

"Friends, that may meet now and then, and feel kindly one toward the other."

His voice was still event in tone - very even, but very distinct and impressive.

At first Irene's face had grown pale, but now a warm flush was pervading it.

"If you desire it, Hartley," she answered, in a voice that trembled in the beginning, but grew firm ere the sentence closed, "it is not for me to say, 'No.' As for kind feelings, they are yours always - always. The bitterness passed from my heart long ago."

"And from mine," said Mr. Emerson.

They were silent for a few moments, and each showed embarrassment.

"Nearly twenty years! That is a long, long time, Irene." His voice showed signs of weakness.

"Yes, it is a long time." It was a mere echo of his words, yet full of meaning.

"Twenty years!" he repeated. "There has been full time for reflection, and, it may be, for repentance. Time for growing wiser and better."

Irene's eyelids drooped until the long lashes lay in a dark fringed line on her pale cheeks. When she lifted them they were wet.

"Yes, Hartley," she answered with much feeling, "there has been, indeed, time for reflection and repentance. It is no light thing to shadow the whole life of a human being."

"As I have shadowed yours."

"No, no," she answered quickly, "I did not mean that; as I have shadowed yours."

She could not veil the tender interest that was in her eyes; would not, perhaps, if it had been in her power.

At this moment a bell rang out clear and loud. Irene started and glanced from the window; then, rising quickly, she said -

"We are at the landing."

There was a hurried passage from cabin to deck, a troubled confusion of thought, a brief period of waiting, and then Irene stood on the shore and Hartley Emerson on the receding vessel. In a few hours miles of space lay between them.

"Irene, darling," said Mrs. Everet, as they met at Ivy Cliff on the next day, "how charming you look! This pure, sweet, bracing air has beautified you like a cosmetic. Your cheeks are warm and your eyes are full of light. It gives me gladness of heart to see in your face something of the old look that faded from it years ago."

Irene drew her arm around her friend and kissed her lovingly.

"Come and sit down here in the library. I have something to tell you," she answered, "that will make your heart beat quicker, as it has mine."

"I have met him," she said, as they sat down and looked again into each other's faces.

"Him! Who?"

"Hartley."

"Your husband?"

"He who was my husband. Met him face to face; touched his hand; listened to his voice; almost felt his heart beat against mine. Oh, Rose darling, it has sent the blood bounding in new life through my veins. He was on the boat yesterday, and came to me as I sat reading. We talked together for a few minutes, when our landing was reached, and we parted. But in those few minutes my poor heart had more happiness than it has known for twenty years. We are at peace. He asked why we might not be as friends who could meet now and then, and feel kindly toward each other? God bless him for the words! After a long, long night of tears, the sweet morning has broken!"

And Irene laid her head down against Rose, hiding her face and weeping from excess of joy.

"What a pure, true, manly face he has!" she continued, looking up with swimming eyes. "How full it is of thought and feeling! You called him my husband just now, Rose. My husband!" The light went back from her face. "Not for time, but -" and she glanced upward, with eyes full of hope - "for the everlasting ages! Oh is it not a great gain to have met here in forgiveness of the past - to have looked kindly into each other's faces - to have spoken words that cannot die?"

What could Rose say to all this? Irene had carried her out of her depth. The even tenor of her life-experiences gave no deep sea-line that could sound these waters. And so she sat silent, bewildered and half afraid.

Margaret came to the library, and, opening the door, looked in. There was a surprised expression on her face.

"What is it?" Irene asked.

"A gentleman has called, Miss Irene."

"A gentleman!"

"Yes, miss; and wants to see you."

"Did he send his name?"

"No, miss."

"Do you know him, Margaret?"

"I can't say, miss, for certain, but - " she stopped.

"But what, Margaret?"

"It may be just my thought, miss; but he looks for all the world as if he might be - "

She paused again.

"Well?"

"I can't say it, Miss Irene, no how, and I won't. But the gentleman asked for you. What shall I tell him?"

"That I will see him in a moment," answered Irene.

Margaret retired.

The face of Irene, which flushed at first, now became pale as ashes. A wild hope trembled in her heart.

"Excuse me for a few minutes," she said to Mrs. Everet, and, rising, left the room.

It was as Irene had supposed. On entering the parlor, a gentleman advanced to meet her, and she stood face to face with Hartley Emerson!

"Irene," he said, extending his hand.

"Hartley," fell in an irrepressible throb from her lips as she put her hand in his.

"I could not return to New York without seeing you again," said Mr. Emerson, as he stood holding the hand of Irene. "We met so briefly, and were thrown apart again so suddenly, that some things I meant to say were left unspoken."

He led her to a seat and sat down beside her, still looking intently in her face. Irene was far from being as calm as when they sat together the day before. A world of new hopes had sprung up in her heart since then. She had lain half asleep and half awake nearly all night, in a kind of delicious dream, from which the morning awoke her with a cold chill of reality. She had dreamed again since the sun had risen; and now the dream was changing into the actual.

"Have I done wrong in this, Irene?" he asked.

And she answered,

"No, it is a pleasure to meet you, Hartley."

She had passed through years of self-discipline, and the power acquired during this time came to her aid. And so she was able to answer with womanly dignity. It was a pleasure to meet him there, and she said so.

"There are some things in the past, Irene," said Mr. Emerson, "of which I must speak, now that I can do so. There are confessions that I wish to make. Will you hear me?"

"Better," answered Irene, "let the dead past bury its dead."

"I do not seek to justify myself, but you, Irene."

"You cannot alter the estimate I have made of my own conduct," she replied. "A bitter stream does not flow from a sweet fountain. That dead, dark, hopeless past! Let it sleep if it will!"

"And what, then, of the future?" asked Mr. Emerson.

"Of the future!" The question startled her. She looked at him with a glance of eager inquiry.

"Yes, of the future, Irene. Shall it be as the past? or have we both come up purified from the fire? Has it consumed the dross, and left only the fine gold? I can believe it in your case, and hope that it is so in mine. But this I do know, Irene: after suffering and trial have done their work of abrasion, and I get down to the pure metal of my heart, I find that your image is fixed there in the imperishable substance. I did not hope to meet you again in this world as now - to look into your face, to hold your hand, to listen to your voice as I have done this day - but I have felt that God was fitting us through earthly trial, for a heavenly union. We shall be one hereafter, dear Irene - one and for ever!"

The strong man broke down. His voice fell into low sobs - tears blinded his vision. He groped about for the hand of Irene, found it, and held it wildly to his lips.

Was it for a loving woman to hold back coldly now? No, no, no! That were impossible.

"My husband!" she said, tenderly and reverently, as she placed her saintly lips on his forehead.

There was a touching ceremonial at Ivy Cliff on the next day - one never to be forgotten by the few who were witnesses. A white-haired minister - the same who, more than twenty years before, had said to Hartley Emerson and Irene Delancy, "May your lives flow together like two pure streams that meet in the same valley," - again joined their hands and called them "husband and wife." The long, dreary, tempestuous night had passed away, and the morning arisen in brightness and beauty.

www.ingramcontent.com/pod-product-compliance
Lightning Source LLC
Chambersburg PA
CBHW030116180626
46812CB00002B/438